PENGUIN BOOKS
HORROR, HE WROTE

Tan Jit Seng is an award-winning creative director of an advertising agency. He started out as the co-creator of Malaysia's first English comic book, *Heroines of Darkness*, and a children's book writer, before publishing a compilation of short stories titled *Get Spooked: Terrifying Tales Untold*. In 2022, he published *Abandoned Gods*, and a year following that, he completed his latest novel, *Horror, He Wrote*.

Horror, He Wrote

The Ladies Under the Bridge

Tan Jit Seng

PENGUIN BOOKS

An imprint of Penguin Random House

PENGUIN BOOKS

Penguin Books is an imprint of the Penguin Random House group of
companies whose addresses can be found at
global.penguinrandomhouse.com

Published by Penguin Random House SEA Pte Ltd
40 Penjuru Lane, #03-12, Block 2
Singapore 609216

First published in Penguin Books by Penguin Random House SEA 2024

ISBN 9789815144796

Typeset in Garamond by MAP Systems, Bengaluru, India

www.penguin.sg

PART I

The Bridge Over Troubled Water

1

'There is nothing to writing,' Ernest Hemingway had said. 'All you have to do is sit at a typewriter and open a vein.' As Ernest Maxwell Graves lay dying in his porcelain bathtub, soaked in the stench of whiskey and failure with his left wrist slit, he was expressly haunted by the worst irony of it all—that a writer of a pedigreed literary lineage such as he, would end up an undignified failure in a forlorn inn at the heart of Maxwell Hill in Taiping, Perak.

It was a cold wet night, brimming with colder regrets. 'Damn the book reviewers,' he groaned bitterly, biting his tongue more in shame than in actual pain.

Their words had cut him like a knife, ridiculing the failure of his latest novel, *Sex and the Pontianak*, which had sold a mere thirteen copies on Amazon and nothing on Kindle. His famous mother, Audrey Kate Graves, the bestselling author of *Intoxi-Kate, the Gothic Vampire*, would turn in her grave were she to read it, the press snickered mercilessly. They went as far as telling him to give up the pen and focus on his 'pen-is' instead, given the fact that he was strikingly good-looking and well-endowed at twenty-seven. He wouldn't succeed without fans, they pointed out gleefully, perhaps he should look for them on OnlyFans, they had suggested in jest.

'Fate be so cruel, the critics worse,' a melodious sing-song voice echoed in the dark of the bathroom, reminiscent of silver bells chiming in the dead of the night over a cemetery, 'I should know.'

Fear rose from his bile and Ernest felt goosebumps prickling his skin; he was frightened more by the spooky encounter than the idea of him dying by suicide. He jolted in his bath, causing the water to splash senselessly and shivered involuntarily thinking this was where the Grim Reaper would take his poor soul. He squinted his eyes to have a better look, expecting to see a hooded skeletal creature with a vicious scythe blade, but all he could see was an apparition of a beautiful Chinese ghost hovering over his cold tiles, her form fluid like a gentle stream shimmering in the moonlight.

'W . . . Who are you?' Ernest asked feebly, his curiosity piqued as he fought for his breath with raspy efforts while feeling his life essence ebbing away. 'Have you come to take me to hell at last?' he asked, hoping for a merciful quick end to his misery.

'I'm Chang Pai Lian, named after the white lotus,' the ghost replied with a smirk, 'and no, I'm not here to bring you to hell. Haven't you got enough of hell already?' She didn't quite want to add to his pain by reminding him that his previous novel, *Howling Pom-Poms*—a story about werewolf cheerleaders—was plagiarized by an adult entertainment company that made millions out of it while he got nothing. When Ernest sued and lost, he had to run away with his tail between his legs from San Francisco to Taiping to avoid paying the legal costs incurred. Who knew a talentless writer like him still had use for bottom feeders? Unfortunately, this next book, *Sex and the Pontianak*, was so bad, no one wanted to steal it even.

'Just let me die,' Ernest begged woefully, ashamed of his non-existent talent and lack of success. 'I am a failure through and through, and have brought much shame to my illustrious family,' he wept in utter embarrassment.

'Not a chance,' the White Lotus ghost insisted while stealing furtive glances at Ernest in the bathtub. She was looking at a possible partner-in-crime, albeit one who was on death's door already. *Don't die just yet*, she implored silently in her heart, hoping he would acquiesce to a mutually beneficial pact with a win-win possibility for all. 'Trust me, you'd want to know about the murder of my twin sister, Chang Hong Lian,' she told him to pique his interest.

Chang Hong Lian? The lady who was dubbed the Red Lotus by the press? Ernest recalled momentarily having read about her murder in the news—her body was found, but her murderer was not.

'You are a writer looking for success and I am a ghost with a story to tell. I can be your ghostwriter if you want,' she told Ernest, and in an instant, it stirred his imagination with a million possibilities.

'Your call,' the White Lotus ghost said as she held up the receiver of the phone on the bathroom wall. 'Shall I dial 999 or 666?' she asked with an enigmatic smile flashing across her face.

Do not cry
By my grave, don't be sad.
I am not on the Taiping bridge,
I have made my bed under it.
I am a thousand regrets deep,
I am the fallen lotus that weeps.
As you walk by the botanical garden,
I am the kiss of the breeze on your cheeks.
Hear the songs of forlorn love birds,
Here I am with tears on my cheeks.
Do not cry
By my grave, don't be sad.
You never loved me, let me be.
Say goodbye, don't be mad.
Wipe your tears, then leave me.

2

The clacking of the typewriter stopped. Reliving her unfortunate love story, the White Lotus ghost burst into tears. The tears from heaven rained on the window, whispering sad nothings into her ears; the flowers in the garden outside the inn swaying in anguish with the cold, cold wind. A nameless writer with the soul of a poet . . . was she not worthy of his love? In life, she was a ghostwriter for a famous crime author, now, an actual ghost writing for someone close to death.

How fate has turned, she thought with a sad sigh, a little lost to the joke that life and death had wrought.

'Do you need a glass of water?' she asked, turning her attention to Ernest when she heard him cough. She paused for an answer but got none. Ernest lay in a deep slumber, exhausted from the long nights at the Taiping Hospital for almost a week where a team of doctors had fought to save his life.

But there was no saving her or her beloved sister, she knew now that they were both dead under the bridge at the Taiping Botanical Garden. She felt heartsick that she would have to recount their painful ordeals all over again. Her sister was murdered, she herself committed suicide. Just how many sins had the bridge witnessed? Just how many secrets did the lotus pond hide? She should have seen the signs . . . It was as clear as a written book!

Her famous lover had committed a heinous murder, thinking he could get away with it. But she could help expose him, damn it! Dead people told no tales, but vengeful souls most definitely did.

By the grace of the Almighty, she would turn this murderer into a rotting corpse by hook or by crook.

Could she bear to turn her beloved in? Could she afford not to when the victim was her own twin sister? All she needed was the perfect opportunity to bring him to justice. It was sheer luck that she bumped into a luckless writer at death's door. She would get to tell her story in his book and he would get a bestseller in return, a win-win situation for both, none would be wiser.

* * *

Tossing and turning in his bed, Ernest Maxwell Graves dreamt of a grieving lady named Chang Pai Lian consumed by a nightmare—her beloved, Adrian Holmes, had committed the perfect murder using the plot of a crime thriller she had ghostwritten for him. The victim? None other than her own twin sister, Chang Hong Lian.

> The winter is here,
> Frozen pond, white lotus sighs . . .
> Knowing it must die.

'The pen is mightier than the sword,' Chang Pai Lian lamented in Ernest's dream, sobbing with much regret, knowing she deserved to die. 'Who knew the pen can also be a borrowed knife?'

> Don't weep, butterfly . . .
> A red lotus lay wilted,
> On a night in spring.

'Blood is on her hands,' Chang Hong Lian cried hysterically as she rose from a pond of red, her accusation sharp like a dagger to her sister's heart, 'and here I was thinking blood is thicker than water!'

Murderer! Murderer! Murderer! Echoes of accusation thundered aloud like rushing waves, crashing onto Adrian Holmes and plunging him into the throes of an underwater whirlpool. The crime novelist's apologies were heard reverberating in the dark abyss, 'I am sorry, I am sorry, I am sorry.'

Ernest jolted up from his troubled slumber. Drenched in cold sweat, his heart raced with dread and anxiety. His unease gave way when he realized he was in his room, comforted by the familiarity of the soft sunlight streaming in from the window and the serenity of the misty hilltop beyond it.

The White Lotus ghost was gone, he noticed, unsure if he should be glad or sad, but then quickly realized that he wasn't even sure if this was all real or only a figment of his imagination. He let out a nervous laugh, but as soon as his eyes met a stack of papers next to his typewriter, all his doubts evaporated.

'It is real!' he exclaimed in utter shock and pounced on it like a cat would on a mouse. With great trepidation, he flipped the pages and realized it was good—bloody good to be exact. Granted that it wasn't entirely complete, but it was already a masterpiece in the making, better than what he could have written in his lifetime. As luck would have it, his 'ghostwriter' was better than so many others . . . alive or dead.

It was a muggy November night. Grief was the torrent of a river down my cheeks and a heart shattered into a million little pieces. Crying at the feet of my twin sister, my sweet, sweet Chang Hong Lian, my precious Red Lotus, I felt my soul dying just looking at her lifeless corpse.

Slain by a nameless vagrant with a fractured mind, her body drowned in the Taiping Botanical Garden's lake, beneath the bridge. The murder weapon was a sharp dagger, found buried in its secret depth, rusted beyond recognition and giving no secrets away—not so much a fingerprint nor any other precious clue.

'No . . .' I wailed, refusing to accept the truth that fate had scripted, protesting against the obvious findings of what would seem like a straightforward case. 'Who takes a stroll in the Taiping Botanical Garden late at night? That too wearing a double-stranded golden pearl necklace from the South Sea, the rarest of the rare in the world, no less! Any sane mind would know it would attract the evils of thieves, and now my sister has paid the ultimate price to an insane man!' I continued inconsolably.

'I am very sorry for your loss, Chang Pai Lian,' an officer from the responding team condoled with me while scribbling something in his notebook. Shaking his head in disbelief at the gruesome murder, he shared his take on the incident. 'Looks like it is an open-and-shut case, the vagrant has admitted to the murder already.'

Days later, it turned out that it was not as straightforward a case as the officer had thought it out to be. My sister was with child.

'W . . . What?!' I became dizzy with shock, blood draining from my face, turning me pallid like a ghost. *Whose child?* I wondered frantically. Then suddenly it struck me, the incident seemed quite familiar, like the plot of a crime thriller . . . Where had I read it? And then I remembered—'I *wrote* it!' I said aloud and the inspector looked at me, baffled. I dashed to the attic where I used to keep stocks of novels I had ghostwritten for authors.

'Here it is, my novel, read it!' I told the officer in manic fervour, almost hyperventilating in my agitated state, while pushing a copy of *A Bridge to Murderville* onto his hands. 'I was a ghostwriter for Adrian Holmes!'

It took weeks for the officer to connect the dots after reading the novel—the main plot was almost parallel to this case. It was the story of an author trying to get rid of his pregnant girlfriend using the borrowed knife tactic—in this case, a random vagrant who had lost his mind used a string of double-stranded pearls as a lure to instigate theft and violence.

'But it doesn't make sense,' I voiced out in all honesty when I met him later. 'Why would someone commit a murder by the book, that too my book?' But per the autopsy report, the DNA results of the child in my sister's womb confirmed Adrian Holmes as the father. The motive? Adrian didn't want his jealous wife, a famous socialite named Marguerite Daisy, to know of his love affair.

Blood left my face, like life had drained my sister's. An affair with my lover, and pregnant at that, imagine!

3

The Indian-Muslim restaurant, or *Mamak* restaurant (as they call it locally), was packed with patrons as usual. Ernest Maxwell Graves had wanted to change the venue last minute but it was too late as Inspector Abdul Rahman, who was now incharge of the case, would be arriving any minute. In any case, A.M. Maju Nasi Kandar restaurant in Lorong Lima, Taiping, was a good choice above many because of its *nasi kandar*, which was great according to local residents.

Seated in a discreet corner while waiting for the man, Ernest sipped his *teh tarik*, or 'pulled tea', a popular hot milk tea found practically anywhere in Malaysia. Its name was derived from the process of repeatedly pouring the drink from one container to another with arms outstretched during preparation, which made it cooler to consume while giving it a layer of froth on top. While he was drinking it, he couldn't help but wonder if someone was pulling his leg. One minute he was at death's door and the next he was being pulled into a murder case with hot leads to share.

Why me? he wondered, not that he was not thankful for the opportunity. His ghostwriter was writing a bestseller for him while he was playing a good Samaritan for the police force. The Inspector had agreed to meet up with him on account that Ernest had some crucial details to the case . . . straight from the horse's mouth, or in this case, a ghost's.

W . . . What if he didn't believe me? Ernest wondered for a bit the possibility of the Inspector discounting his 'evidence'. Well, this would all be a waste of time, but hey, he was doing what anyone in his circumstances would have done. Whether the Inspector appreciated his efforts or not, it didn't matter, he would be giving the man a brown envelope containing photocopies of the pages the White Lotus ghost had typed to help with the case anyway.

'Are you okay?' Inspector Abdul Rahman asked the man in front of him, correctly surmising the sole Caucasian man to be Ernest, waking the latter from his reverie.

With a strained huff, the Inspector pulled a chair to park his heavy ass on. 'I suppose you're the one with new leads for Chang Hong Lian's murder case?' he asked Ernest before beckoning the waiter to take his order, 'I am famished. Let's get something good to eat. What will you have?'

'I do have information about the case and I think you would be duly surprised,' Ernest replied before asking him, 'What's good here besides *nasi kandar*?' He didn't quite fancy lining up for the spicy dishes displayed at the food counter. In any case, he wasn't about to leave the table with his precious brown envelope on it.

'He will have the mutton biryani, the same as me,' Inspector Abdul Rahman told the waiter, ordering on Ernest's behalf since the *ang mo* didn't know what to have for lunch. 'Talk,' the Inspector said to Ernest, 'I only came here because you said you have information regarding this case.'

'I was visited by Chang Pai Lian last night,' Ernest confessed, eager to see the Inspector's reaction while watching the waiter coming back to their table with their orders. As expected, the Inspector looked at him like he was some kind of a mental case before sighing regretfully.

'I knew I shouldn't have come. What a waste of my time!' Inspector Abdul Rahman thundered angrily before tucking into his meal. 'Chang Pai Lian is dead! She committed suicide early this month by jumping off the bridge in Taiping Botanical Garden, right at the spot where her twin sister, Chang Hong Lian, had died over a month ago.'

You'd know this if you had read the news, the Inspector seethed inside, *it was all over the media if you cared to know.* Eyeing Ernest suspiciously, he wondered for a moment what the latter would say for himself. *It had better be good, damn it!*

'I didn't say she visited me in person,' Ernest said with a smile as he took the first bite of his biryani. 'She visited me in her spirit form.' Looking at the flabbergasted inspector, he added, 'Yes, as in a ghost. *Hantu* in your language!'

'W—What?!' the startled inspector bellowed, almost choking on a piece of mutton in his throat upon hearing it. This was most unusual, to say the least. *Perhaps there is more than meets the eye*, his mind raced to comprehend. 'Did she say anything to you?'

'No, but she wrote about it,' Ernest said, pushing the brown envelope containing photocopies of the incomplete manuscript towards him. 'She died an unfortunate death and wants the world to know what Adrian Holmes did to her sister.'

Is this guy pulling my leg with the story of a ghost? The Inspector baulked at the envelope.

But the incomplete manuscript needed to be looked into, and if it did check out, he would be on a roll. Imagine the leads he could pursue, from the first-hand insights of a ghost, one so close to the deceased! An unconventional source of information for sure, but no one needed to know right? Imagine how fast he could close this case and get the promotion he had always wanted!

'Keep me informed,' said the Inspector, not discounting Graves' story for the moment. Real or not, he wasn't about to look a gift horse in the mouth, or in this case, a ghost, and a very gifted one at that. Smelling an opportunity for fame and success, he had decided to look into this case personally, wrestling it from the responding officer. 'I could easily verify the details in the course of my investigation,' he said knowing fully well that he had the resources to do just that.

'Okay,' Ernest replied. He was only doing this to help Chang Pai Lian. The more information she gave them, the faster the murderer could be convicted in court. Seeing this as an opportune moment, he asked the Inspector, 'Has the murderer been apprehended?'

'As you probably have heard by now, we had to send the crazy vagrant from the Taiping Botanical Garden to the Taiping Hospital for psychiatric evaluation,' the Inspector said as he gestured to the waiter to order another drink. 'But as fate would have it, the van overturned, and the crazy man escaped custody.'

'*Satu Teh O Limau Ais*,' he said, ordering an iced tea with lemon and no sugar, as he scooped some *sambal* onto the briyani rice before resuming his conversation with Ernest. 'As for Adrian Holmes, we are currently holding him in a prison cell for the time being to help out with the investigation.'

'Do you think these two have a connection?' Ernest asked when he felt all this was too convenient. The homeless vagrant had admitted freely to the murder. Yet Adrian was implicated by Chang Pai Lian before she conveniently committed suicide. Many things didn't quite add up.

'We'll find out sooner or later,' the Inspector assured Ernest as he handed the latter his name card. He wanted to scare Ernest witless by asking him not to leave town but that would be too cruel a prank. Besides, he needed an unwitting informant, one with close ties to the ghost. 'We're going to work together very closely. You inform me whatever Pai Lian writes and I'll investigate the details,' he said with a smile and a wink.

I am the dying monstress,
Crying under his bed,
Beneath the soft mattress,
Where nightmares are fed.
Where is she, the wife cries,
Every word he says is a lie,
Monstress under the bed cries,
Every day I feel myself die.

Throughout our affair, Adrian Holmes behaved in a strange, aloof manner—like he didn't care to know me as a person, although he sure did since I was the one who wrote his books. Sometimes, when he was at my house, I would notice he had this strange habit of looking at my wall clock as he undressed. That scared me and made me nervous. I hated the clock, never once looking at it while he was there because he would be off in an hour or two and I didn't want to waste borrowed time.

Is it his way of letting me know that he has to be back for dinner with his wife, I wondered?

Still, this love could go on and on if I didn't rock the boat, never once asking him to go yachting in Sipadan Island, Sabah, or cruising in Ibiza, Spain.

I could go on and on, this long wait for him to leave his wife; I would even endure the 'no phone-call' rule. Then one day, I received a bouquet of white lotuses sent to me—blooms of my namesake—acknowledging our love with the words, *I love you, Chang Pai Lian.*

And I cried, remembering why I had endured so much pain for this love.

4

Tears of sadness flowed. *This is madness*, the White Lotus ghost thought, recollecting the love and the pain she had endured. Had she lived her life just to feel this pain? Why did it hurt so badly even after she had died?

Brushing away her tears, she tidied up the table and compiled the latest chapters in a neat order so Ernest could read them later. With loving care, she placed it next to the typewriter where he could find it easily.

'Amazing! The clacking of the typewriter all night didn't wake him up,' the White Lotus ghost muttered sardonically, thinking Ernest was one of those people who could sleep through a storm or a poltergeist outbreak. She turned to look at him disapprovingly for ignoring her presence and suddenly remembered something from her past . . . the times she'd been ignored by Adrian Holmes.

If her memory served her right, Adrian had been on his mobile phone all night. It was just an ordinary weeknight dinner, nothing extraordinary, no celebration of any sort. She had prepared some wonton dumpling soup, spicy-sweet General Tso's chicken, honey walnut tofu, and Szechuan shrimp with red pepper.

Adrian hadn't touched any of the dishes but had been constantly texting someone on the phone. *Is it his wife?* she had wondered. Feeling a little jealous, she had let her cutlery do the talking on her plate—the clinking of the spoon and the clanking of the fork—her silence as explosive as the protest in her heart. She had been trying hard to swallow food and pride, she remembered vaguely.

'Can you stop that, Hong . . . Pai Lian?' Adrian had snapped irritably, quick enough to halt the Freudian slip of his tongue . . . but a mistake nonetheless that spoke volumes. The White Lotus ghost had thought she had caught it but wasn't too sure if she had misheard her own name. If she had pursued it, he would have deemed her irrational and would have left in a huff, slamming the door. 'I'm trying to talk to my brother,' he had said.

Brother? Since when did Adrian have a brother? she had wondered. If he had, he certainly hadn't told her that was for sure. Another Freudian slip perhaps, maybe even a lie to cover up something he didn't want her to know.

'Eat up,' she had urged him, trying to diffuse the situation. Struggling hard not to cry in front of him and cause a scene, she had got up saying, 'I'll do the dishes,' and walked into the kitchen.

In response, she had heard the front door close while she was busy cleaning up and only then had she allowed herself to cry her heart out.

5

The Taiping Prison was the oldest correctional facility in Malaysia, built in 1879 by prisoners of war and convicts brought in from India and Africa. Just a few weeks ago, Adrian Holmes was brought in to be incarcerated while awaiting his trial for the murder of Chang Hong Lian, who was dubbed as Red Lotus by the press. The scandal of a great crime writer was too good for the paparazzi to pass and they didn't shy away from pointing out the fact that the Taiping Prison was just a stone's throw away from the scene of the crime—the Taiping Botanical Garden—causing more humiliation to an already distressed Adrian.

'Cut the crap, your apologies mean nothing to me,' Marguerite Daisy Holmes snapped at her husband from the other side of the tempered glass in the visitation hall, her perfectly manicured nails gripping the handle of the phone like she was about to fling it at him—she would have done a Naomi Campbell had it not been for the barrier between them, such was her fury. 'You no-good sorry excuse of a husband, you frigging deserve what's coming for you!' she spat out choice words, causing red burns on the ears of the prison officers upon hearing their quarrel outside the door.

'Calm down, Marguerite,' Adrian begged his wife, heartbroken at the sorry state he was in—his wife mad at his betrayal, both of his mistresses dead, and he himself looking at the death penalty if convicted. 'Trust me, baby, I didn't kill Hong Lian, why wouldn't you believe me?' he cried his heart out, his proclamation of innocence falling on deaf ears.

'Don't you baby, baby me!' his wife screamed vehemently, her well-preserved face almost contorted with rage despite the Botox injections she had just had. 'You had a baby with her!'

He bit his lips, preferring to confess nothing for the moment. So far, his wife knew only of his one mistress—Hong Lian— ignorant of the fact that he had bedded the other twin, Pai Lian, as well. Thankfully, Marguerite didn't have the presence of mind to check under her bed for Pai Lian the last time she had tried catching them together.

To the best of his knowledge, the affair was kept such a secret that even Pai Lian didn't know he had slept with Hong Lian and impregnated her. It would kill Pai Lian if she did.

'I am really, really sorry, I truly am. What I did was wrong of me,' Adrian apologized again but to no avail. 'Hope you will forgive me over time, but I really didn't commit the crime,' he asserted again and again, not that it mattered to Marguerite Daisy anyhow—not anymore—seeing that he would be put to death if convicted.

'You had the cheek to steal my South Sea pearl necklace and give it to your mistress,' his wife accused him, her eyes tearing at the thought that nothing was sacred to her philandering husband . . . not her bed, not her jewellery. 'Just frigging give it back to me because it was an inheritance from my late mother!'

'I didn't steal it, I swear!' Adrian said, hurt beyond words that his wife would think he did such a thing. A philanderer he might be but a thief he was not, or so he maintained despite his wife thinking otherwise. Then, he paused for a moment, struggling with the distinct feeling that his wife was putting up an act but he quickly dismissed the doubts because he was in the heat of an argument.

'Then who did?' Marguerite Daisy shouted back, fuming that her husband was still trying to keep up his pretences. 'Oh, just drop it, stop lying!' she snapped at him irritably, thinking it was a mistake visiting him in prison. She should have just left him to rot here, the precious double-stranded pearl necklace would find its way back to her, one way or another, it always did. 'You stole my pearl necklace and you gave it to your mistress,' she accused him again, making sure it was loud enough for the prison guards to hear.

'No, I really didn't,' Adrian said and wept, knowing in his heart that no matter what he said now, he would never be believed, not after what he had done. All this happened because of love affairs that had gone wrong, and the price of rapture's due might have to be paid with his life. How hopeless he felt now, like being dragged six feet under to his death, a deserving end scripted by fate for crimes that he insisted he hadn't committed. Having said that, he could not have written a better ending if he tried, save maybe for Chang Pai Lian.

Wait a minute, he thought and felt a sense of unease, like he was reliving the plot from *A Bridge to Murderville*, which he had got it ghostwritten in 1968. *How strange, life imitates art*, he thought and shuddered at the sheer coincidence of it. Or was it?

'Hmm . . . I have been set up,' he decided on his innocence, the writer in him trying to rewrite his fate. 'It cannot end this way for me.'

Who was the only woman he brought to his marital bed? Pai Lian! He would have forgotten this incident had his wife, Marguerite, not stormed into their bedroom and created a scene.

Was it then that Pai Lian stole his wife's precious pearls? If so, why? It couldn't have been Hong Lian—she was relegated to cheap motel rooms when it came to their forbidden trysts, if his memory had served him right.

'Listen! I've been set up!' He screamed in anguish to his wife who was momentarily taken aback by his sudden impassioned reaction. 'You have to help me, Marguerite! This is all Pai Lian's doing!'

'Who is Pai Lian?' Marguerite Daisy asked Adrian point-blank, afraid of his answer. *Another one! So, the whore had a name after all,* she thought angrily. Her eyes went dead like her heart, and then without hesitation, she spat her venom at his face, 'Is she one of your mistresses?'

'I . . . er . . . I,' words failed Adrian at his blunder, confirming Marguerite Daisy's worst fear. His mind went into turmoil like the emotions in his heart. It was Pai Lian, wasn't it? Or was it the other twin he had inadvertently brought into his home? At times, he couldn't tell the twins apart, to be honest—a side chick was a side chick to him, nothing more.

But how would one explain the fact that Hong Lian was the one who wore his wife's precious South Sea pearls on the night of her murder then? 'I . . . I . . . really don't know what to say,' he said in a pitiful voice, feeling defeated and at a loss for words. Things had escalated to such an unfortunate state that he didn't really know what to think anymore.

'I think you are in denial,' Marguerite Daisy said and cried with bitterness, 'that you would grasp at straws to save your own damn skin.' Never mind that her husband would be put to death upon conviction in a few months' time; she was already dead inside now.

She stood up and took a deep breath to calm her nerves, and just before she took her leave, she gave a scathing parting shot, 'Goodbye, Adrian, may you rot in hell with your whores for all of eternity!'

No sooner had the curse left her mouth, Adrian Holmes suddenly went ballistic, 'It is you, isn't it? You want me dead so you can inherit my fortune!'

Stop all the clocks, stop the march of time,
Prevent my eyes from making so much rain.
Cut off the telephone, cut this life of mine,
Buy me a coffin and bury me with my pain.
Stop the stars from shining, stop all their lights,
Pour away the seas and kiss the fishes bye-bye.
Die with the waning moon, die I will tonight,
My ocean of grief is deep so kiss me goodbye.

I . . . I wanted to die. Since my twin sister's tragic passing, my days were a blur, oftentimes I couldn't remember what transpired between the setting of the sun and the rising of the moon or between the nightmares and the sleepless nights. I was dying inside, crying, bleeding, screaming at the demise of my twin sister at the hands of my lover; angry and hurt at everything and anything; at myself for not doing enough and at God for letting it happen.

Guilt had made me feel like I had killed my own sister. My own words in my lover's books had found life to end my sister's soul, verily giving ideas to my hateful crime novelist of an ex-lover to do the dastardly deed. I clawed at my own breasts on the nights I lost my sanity and reason, hoping the cage of my heart would break open to release the torrent of unbearable grief that I had to endure.

Damn you, Adrian Holmes. You murdered my twin sister, and in some way, you killed me too. You effectively took my soul and now I am a goner in more ways than one. Dead I might be under the same bridge that my twin sister had died. But mark the words of a dead woman . . . crime doesn't pay! I will make sure you face justice and pay for all your crimes . . . in one way or another!

6

Tears flowed down Ernest's cheeks when he read the heart-rending poem from the latest chapter of Chang Pai Lian's manuscript. The immense pain in her heart was so overwhelming that she couldn't see a way out but to end her life; forever meant nothing to her soul, not nearly enough for her tears that carelessly stained the ground. *How much more could a poor girl like her take from life? When the pain came in torrents of waves that threatened to pull her sanity under, no respite to catch her breath?* he thought to himself.

Damn Adrian Holmes! Murder, murder, evil crime . . . wicked, wicked, do your time! It was murder by the book literally and that made it so much easier for Inspector Abdul Rahman to bring the culprit to book—with a court warrant—even though the latter had used a borrowed knife to do the terrible deed, in this instance a nameless and witless vagrant. It was an open-and-shut case and it would take no time for the authorities to bring it to a close, surely.

It was beyond Ernest how anyone could have the heart to murder a mother and child in cold blood. He didn't really like to judge a book by its cover, but heck! Adrian Holmes, the bestselling crime novelist, certainly looked the part of a murderer in a handsome, dangerous kind of way . . . a heartless cad with a tad of charm; no, make that a ton of charm. Why did women always fall for the bad boys anyway? Where did that leave the good boys that only their mothers could love?

Ahh . . . the thought left a trail of warm tears on his cheeks again. He missed his late mother, Audrey Kate Graves, dearly.

She was a celebrated author who wrote horror books that rivalled Anne Rice's. Who could forget her first novel, *Intoxi-Kate, the Gothic Vampire*? It was a bestseller right off the printing press. While Ernest's books were criticized by the press, each of Audrey's books, including *Raising Medusa, Goddess in Control, The Canterbury Siren,* and *The Devil's Daughter*, had made it to bestsellers' lists. Even more impressive was the fact that she was the recipient of three Booker Prizes!

If Chang Pai Lian can make it here from beyond, can my late mother not come too? he wondered sometimes. He could really do with his mother's loving presence right about now. A mother's love was something of a mystery that no one could really explain; it encompassed deep devotion, sacrifice, and pain that were as endless as love was unselfish and enduring. Surely she would come to save him if he came to any harm.

Then, by chance, something interesting in Pai Lian's manuscript caught his eyes and made him jump. Apparently, Adrian Holmes had signed a pre-nuptial agreement with Marguerite Daisy—in the event of infidelity, his wife would inherit all his money. If he couldn't get the itch out of his pants, a lot of money would spill out of his pockets—his $100 million to be exact—to his wife.

There was a brief mention of his lawyer's name, a certain Jasmine Somasundram, a friend of Marguerite Daisy who had drafted the pre-nuptial agreement, ironclad it seemed. Hmm . . . could it be that his wife was working with this lawyer? No, it couldn't be. She came across as the poor victim in the press, the wife wronged by the philandering husband.

Anyway, that pre-nuptial agreement was motive enough to commit a murder and erase all evidence, no? Well, in the eyes of the law, it was certainly so, and Adrian was incarcerated as a result. But was that all there was to it? Ernest couldn't help but think there was more to this. *It can't be this simple, could it?* he pondered.

Who would be stupid enough to commit a murder by the book, as Chang Pai Lian had pointed out, word for word, plot for plot? That was crazy! It felt like it was some kind of a set up, too convenient if truth be told.

But what if it was? Who knew the book so well enough to do it? Chang Pai Lian, the ghostwriter? How ridiculous, that thought! *She has already died for goodness' sake, she is out of the equation*, he chastised himself. Lest he forget, she had saved him from a certain death and was writing a bestseller for him. *Slap, slap, slap!* Ernest walloped his own face, he certainly deserved to be whacked for questioning his benefactor.

Was this all the homeless vagrant's doing then? A pregnant Chang Hong Lian murdered as a result of being at the wrong place at the wrong time? Why had she worn a pearl necklace to the botanical garden in the middle of the night? Was she meeting someone? If she was, who was it? Had the responding officer even tried to find out? No, the latter had just apprehended the homeless vagrant after that halfwit admitted to the murder, but that lucky sod had escaped custody when the van overturned. Current whereabouts, unknown.

Ding dong, went the doorbell, which startled Ernest from his thoughts. He left aside the manuscript and headed for the room door before stopping short in his tracks for a brief second—he was still wearing his white briefs from yesterday and wondered if he should answer the door in it. Nahhh . . . he had better not. He slipped on the hotel bathrobe that he grabbed from the closet and walked to the door.

'Who is it?' he asked and peered into the glass peephole on his door that gave a fish-eye view of whoever was on the other side. It turned out to be Inspector Abdul Rahman. *This must be urgent*, Ernest thought, *having the man himself paying him a visit in his suite at the inn.* They had only met a couple days back and hadn't planned on meeting again so soon.

With much curiosity, he half-opened his room door that was securely latched by the door chain and peering from the side gap, he asked, 'Oh, it's you. How can I help you?'

'There has been some development, Ernest,' Inspector Abdul Rahman said to him, fidgeting uncomfortably at first but he had to say what he had come here to say, albeit a bit reluctantly, 'The chapters you shared with me checked out. Let me in.'

Upon hearing that, an excited Ernest unlocked the latch-chain and let the Inspector in. Seeing the disapproving look on the Inspector's face when he saw him in a bathrobe, Ernest sighed and said resignedly, 'I'll go change, make yourself at home.'

As Ernest made his way into his bedroom to change into something more presentable, Inspector Abdul Rahman wandered about in the living room and chanced upon the former's typewriter and the manuscript by the table. *Good! More chapters mean more revelation,* he thought gleefully to himself, *I'll be able to close the case faster and earn my well-deserved promotion.*

Without meaning to, he gave furtive glances at the corners of the hotel suite, hoping to catch a glimpse or two of the White Lotus ghost, but alas, he didn't see her and was more than a little disappointed. Did he feel a cold spot in the room? Nope, he didn't, but if there was one, it would have been negated by the air-conditioner anyway. Did he feel a presence in the room? Nope, he didn't. But if he did sense something later, he was sure he would brag about it in the office.

'What can I offer you?' Ernest asked the Inspector from behind as he adjusted his T-shirt over his blue denim jeans, startling the jittery man who jumped as though he had seen a ghost. To be honest, Ernest felt the man had come here for another reason, probably to satiate his curiosity and check out the White Lotus ghost for himself, rather than wanting to share updates with him. Good luck with that pretext, Chang Pai Lian hadn't manifested to anyone else but him. 'There are drinks and snacks in the mini bar,' he said invitingly to the Inspector, knowing the latter wouldn't resist some refreshments.

'A Diet Coke please,' Inspector Abdul Rahman replied. His choice of beverage made Ernest roll his eyes. *The man is probably trying to lose weight but has failed miserably. It would have been fine had he been honest and asked for just Coke—no shame in admitting one has lost one's fight really,* Ernest thought as he went to the mini bar. 'And all the chocolates and nuts you have in the mini bar, if you please.'

'O . . . Okay,' a surprised Ernest said with raised eyebrows, and picked everything from the mini bar and placed it onto the coffee table where the Inspector had taken his seat on the plush sofa.

'I'm so very glad the manuscript's all verified; that's reassurance we haven't been lied to.'

'But the prosecution team wanted us to prove there's a link between Adrian Holmes and the homeless vagrant; otherwise, it would be circumstantial evidence,' Inspector Abdul Rahman told Ernest. If they failed to prove it, chances were that Adrian would get a mistrial and he could get away scot-free, like the homeless vagrant who had escaped custody. This would be tantamount to judicial failure and a big waste of time and taxpayers' money. 'I came here to see if you can ask your ghost if she knew there was a connection.'

'I don't know if it works that way, but I can try,' Ernest said to the Inspector. Yes, he had spoken to the ghost directly before but she had always kept to herself while writing the book.

Talking about books, wasn't there something about a connection between the real killer and his borrowed knife in Pai Lian's book? Maybe Inspector Abdul Rahman should read *A Bridge to Murderville* to find the correlation. 'In the meantime, our White Lotus ghost has completed a few more new chapters. I'll send the photocopies to you in a day or two.'

'No need, I've brought my camera. May I?' the Inspector asked before brandishing a police-issued gadget from his pocket while walking towards the table with the work-in-progress manuscript. Ernest took the hint and walked along with the man and rearranged the pages to ensure they were in order before being photographed for evidence. As flashes of light bombarded the room, the Inspector asked, 'Do you think Pai

Lian knew about Hong Lian's pregnancy before or after her twin
sister got murdered?'

Even before Ernest got to speak, the bottle of Diet Coke
on the coffee table unexpectedly shattered into smithereens,
sending chills down their spines and causing an awkward silence
to permeate the room.

Her emotions ebb and flow.
Waves of blood engulf her soul.
Her life cut, head suffers a blow.
Pearls stolen, a crime most foul.
Under the bridge, a lotus dies.
Looking for love on the wrong side.
Over the bridge, my grief dries.
Don't be lonely, I'll join your side.

In less time than it took to think, with less tears than it took to dry, I, Chang Pai Lian, decided to end it all and join my sister under the bridge where the lotuses of our namesakes bloomed and died. We came from the same womb, it was only right that we shared the same tomb, I reasoned. In any case, I was tired of living in loneliness, weary of my burdens and sick of my guilt.

Breathe! My instincts urged me, *just breathe and live,* and I said, *No! How can I breathe when I am drowning?* I questioned the voices in my head. It felt more like drowning in thoughts than in water if truth be told, my emotions crashing over me like the waves of a pond in a terrible storm.

Oh, damn the flood of confusion distressing my soul! My mind swimming in guilt, my heart beating like a drum—tides of anxiety rising and panic crashing my consciousness just before a strange calmness overwhelmed me. Then death took over, my soul drifting away from my body in a languid sweep.

For a moment, I felt a much-needed release from within me—that very relief I had yearned for, which had alluded me for so long, was now mine to savour and appreciate.

But alas, it didn't last! I didn't see my sister, Chang Hong Lian, waiting for me with open arms and my heart broke with grief. *Where are you, my beloved Red Lotus?* I cried aloud, hoping for echoes of my sadness to reach her ears. Nothing, only the silence of her absence deepened with the wounds in my heart. Flickers of guilt for the loss of her life rekindled regret in me for all the things that were left unsaid or undone when she was alive, with me.

Where is heaven, where is hell? I wondered. Anything would be better than being lonely in the afterlife, especially after suffering so much of loneliness in my life.

I rose from the lake and sat on a nearby park bench while looking at the raintrees swaying in distress caused by the onslaught of the late-year monsoon. Here, there was no danger of anyone running into me and getting shocked by my unearthly ghostly presence, not in this kind of storm I would say.

It gave me time to think, now that I was denied entry into heaven or hell, I must ponder on what to do next. I recalled the wisdom of the ages, of old wives' tale and ancient beliefs, that a ghost would find no release until he or she has completed what must be done.

And I knew what I must do—avenge my sister's death by bringing her real murderer to justice. How would I do that? By writing about her story for the world to know. The irony didn't fly past me. I was a ghostwriter in life and now in death, only this time I would be writing a horror book, not a crime novel—just to expose all of Adrian Holmes' evil doings and give him hell!

7

'Oh, Pai Lian, you are here,' Ernest acknowledged the White Lotus ghost's presence, waking up suddenly from his night rest. With a yawn, he sat on the edge of his bed, his warm blanket sliding down to his hips—revealing his ill choice of Mickey Mouse pyjamas. *What's next, Sailor Moon jammies?* the ghost wondered at his questionable attire. *Some boys never grow up,* she groaned inwardly, thinking this was why ghosts preferred invisibility.

'Oh, you've been very busy,' Ernest noted brightly, looking at the piles of chapters on the table. At the rate things were going, Inspector Abdul Rahman would be most pleased, the case could be closed sooner than he had thought. The Inspector wouldn't be the only one happy, Ernest would be too. He would get his bestseller at last!

'Oh, did I wake you?' the ghost asked Ernest coyly, clacking the last full stop on the page she was writing. 'It won't be long before it is completed,' she assured him, smiling brightly to ease the awkward situation in case he got freaked out by her unearthly apparition.

'Great!' Ernest exclaimed and jumped up in joy upon hearing the good news, his blanket dropping to the ground, giving the White Lotus ghost an eyeful of Mickey Mouse celebrating a party or something with Minnie Mouse, oh dear! The birthday cakes, balloons, and confetti. The designer must have died and gone to hell.

'C . . . Can I ask you about something?' Ernest said to the White Lotus ghost, remembering what Inspector Abdul Rahman had asked him to do. Should he broach the subject about the homeless vagrant? The one who murdered her twin sister? He might as well, what harm could a question like this pose?

'Do you know anything about the homeless vagrant who killed Hong Lian?'

The shocked expression on the face of the White Lotus ghost confused Ernest, especially the part when she accidentally muttered, 'Did I miss something?' while looking a little frantic.

'N . . . No, I don't believe I do,' she replied and smiled while a thousand questions tore her mind. They must be looking for a correlation, she surmised. Was Adrian going to escape justice? No way in hell, she vowed. 'But in the book I wrote for Adrian Holmes, the killer and his borrowed knife were related.'

Ernest paused for a while, not knowing what to think or say. Did he accidentally upset his benefactor? This would make the second question even harder, and he was sure the White Lotus ghost wouldn't like it one bit.

'E . . . Err . . . When did you know your sister was pregnant? Was it before or after she had died?' He asked, hoping it wouldn't jeopardize their partnership. If Inspector Abdul Rahman wanted to know this, it was probably important to the case.

Tears flowed freely from the White Lotus ghost, her disappointment in Ernest visible on her face. Nobody knew her heart was empty, all her emotions gone with her sister, for she wore a smile to brave her days. Nobody knew she was crying inside out, and nobody needed to know.

'I . . . I will take my leave for now,' the White Lotus ghost told Ernest sadly, refusing to answer his question for now. There would be a time for that, but she needed to get herself together first. Why didn't they ask if she was guilty of killing her sister instead? Why didn't they ask why she killed herself before the investigation was over if they wanted to know?

'Don't go!' Ernest begged desperately but the ghost had already made a hasty exit through the wall, disappearing with a quiet whisper, much to his disappointment. It was both questions that had spooked the White Lotus ghost, Ernest confirmed sadly although he didn't really know why.

Oh God, he hoped to heaven that this incident didn't affect their partnership adversely.

8

14 December 1979

'The mountain has its gold, the sky has its stars,' Marguerite Daisy Holmes said to no one in particular as she caressed her string of South Sea pearl necklace in her hands. 'And I have my pearls from the ocean . . . finally.' It wasn't just any pearl necklace—it was a double-stranded masterpiece with the rarest of pearls that gave off a golden hue, all procured from the Celebes Sea between Indonesia and the Philippines. Only the gold-lipped Pinctada Maxima oysters produced such treasures, and hers was strung together with silken threads of actual gold. Apparently, these golden ones were even more precious than the black pearls themselves, worth at least $50 million in total when the necklace was last appraised by Sotheby's in Paris, back in 1953.

Earlier that day, Inspector Abdul Rahman had returned the evidence to her by court order because she could prove it was hers by showing them the will that her mother had left her.

In fact, he was so friendly that he had personally gone to return her jewellery in her holiday bungalow in Kamunting, an upscale hilly residential address in the heart of Taiping, Perak. That visit had brought her surprising news as well—her husband had sought a lawyer's services to write her off from his will.

'He thinks I am responsible for his plight,' Marguerite Daisy contemplated her predicament, anger rising when she thought of the anguish he had brought into her life, 'He sought to punish me, that bastard!'

Her man was a pain in the ass; firstly because of his philandering ways, and secondly, he was about to deny her a $100 million fortune after his death. Never mind that there were legal avenues for her to contest his will on grounds that she was still very much his legally wedded wife. If push came to shove, she was not averse to spilling his dirty linen all over the tabloids.

Having an extramarital affair was ground for a divorce, and being convicted of multiple ones would inflict serious dents on his coffers.

A divorce gets me about 50 per cent of his wealth, she summed up the math in her mind, *a death gets me a 100 per cent of his total net worth.* It was plain as day that she would be better off with him dead in a coffin if she were to benefit from everything he had owned.

Best of all? She didn't have to do it herself—the Malaysian Government would do all the work on account of his heinous crimes.

'But I am not a woman to be trifled with,' she declared angrily, spite screaming in her heart.

She was scorned, the one left behind for mistresses, and she was terribly pissed to say the least. In her agitated state of mind, she could imagine the devil on her left shoulder screaming for revenge while the angel on her right pleaded for mercy.

How ludicrous! Of course she would teach the bastard a lesson that he would never forget, and his whores as well for ruining her marriage. If he didn't love her, why should she care for his feelings at all? At the end of the day, it was about self-preservation—she wanted what was rightfully hers by marriage. 'I will *not* be written out of his will,' she swore, resolute in her conviction to get all that he had for putting her through hell in their marriage. 'I would sooner see him dead myself than lose what's legally mine now!'

'Are you ready?' A voice interrupted Marguerite Daisy's daydreaming, jolting her back to reality. It was Lady Nightshade, a psychic medium of Romani descent whom she had hired all the way from New Orleans to hold a seance to contact her mother from the spiritual realm. She was a little on the heavy side but a true heavy weight when it came to all things occult.

'Have you got your mother's pearl necklace with you, dearie?' Lady Nightshade asked as she prepared the mysterious ritual supplies on the table—thirteen violet candles, a crystal ball, and some cinnamon-scented incense—before switching on some incantation music in preparation of the paranormal visitation.

'I am ready,' Marguerite Daisy replied, and took her place by the table. She carefully placed the precious golden South Sea pearl necklace on the elegant Fenteer black velvet necklace display set and asked Lady Nightshade, 'My mother will come, right? I need her advice on how to deal with my husband right now.'

Madam Petunia Yates may have been dead for decades now, but every now and then she would visit her daughter, Marguerite Daisy, from beyond her grave to give her two cents' worth of advice when summoned by a psychic—usually helping out with the latter's many marriage woes and to dispense questionable beauty tips; never mind the dead woman could never hold a decent relationship when she was alive or her fashion sense came from the now defunct *Le Moniteir De La Mode* magazine.

'We can begin the seance, and don't worry, she will be there for you like always,' Lady Nightshade reassured Marguerite Daisy as she placed the urn containing the old lady's ashes in the middle of the table and scattered some fresh petunias around it for good measure, 'Let's hold hands and touch the pearl necklace to summon her.'

'*Vino de acolo, te chem*, Come from yonder, I summon you,' Lady Nightshade began the proceeding by reciting her spell, as calm overtook chaos and restlessness gave way to rest. A breeze slowly stirred, bringing along with it the scent of petunias, '*Iesiti doamna* Petunia Yates, *mama lui* Marguerite Daisy; Come forth Petunia Yates, mother of Marguerite Daisy,'

'Are you there, mama dear?' Marguerite Daisy asked, feeling a presence in the room as the flame on the candle next to her stirred with life. She might not know the art of scrying but she could clearly make out a vision of what looked like a petunia in full bloom emerging on the haphazard crystalline formations from within the spherical ball in her current state of mind. 'Ahh . . . mummy dearest, you are here,' Marguerite muttered under her breath, feeling warm and fuzzy inside now that her mother had come to her in her hour of need.

'*Astepta! Ceva este ingrozitor de gresit!*' Lady Nightshade cried in alarm, sensing something had gone terribly wrong. In less time than it took for the crow to caw, the psychic medium was possessed in body and spirit, clawing at her hair in agony, 'Marguerite Daisy! Run now, my sweetest daughter, you are in terrible danger!'

Then, it happened, the hostile takeover—the possession of a soul by another spirit—this one a malevolent entity, its identity was clear to those in the know. Like a sick cat coughing up a hairball, Lady Nightshade vomited red lotus petals stained with blood while her crystal ball projected a vision of a red lotus bleeding.

'Hello, Marguerite Daisy, we meet at last. I am Red Lotus, but you can call me Hong Lian,' a possessed Lady Nightshade shrieked dramatically while protesting the hostile takeover of her soul with all the strength she could muster. With the crackling of bones heard loud and clear, Lady Nightshade stumbled painfully towards a shocked Marguerite Daisy and taunted the latter against her will, 'I am here for my pearl necklace!'

'It's mine!' Marguerite Daisy snapped vehemently, tearing up with hatred and pain as she grabbed the pearl necklace from the Fenteer necklace display set and kept it close to her bosom. The nerve this ghost had, first stealing her husband and now this. 'It's my family heirloom!'

'You lie!' the ghost thundered in denial, her grief overwhelming her. Those tears she had shed for her lover would never go away; this unending pain in her heart would haunt her forever to the end of days. 'My sister, Chang Pai Lian, gave it to me,' the ghost revealed with great sadness in her voice, 'On the night I told her I was with Adrian's child.'

Something clicked in Marguerite Daisy's mind. What if it was all true? What if Pai Lian had somehow stolen her necklace? Only to give it to her twin sister, Hong Lian, and send the latter to her death? Was she smelling revenge? It wasn't incomprehensible to imagine jealousy playing a part in this story. The scandal of Pai Lian's own twin sister having an affair with her own lover would be too much to bear . . . let alone hearing the news that Hong Lian was bearing Adrian's love child!

'You've got it so wrong,' Marguerite Daisy told the ghost, trying her best to explain the situation. Failure to do so would be disastrous for her and her psychic medium, she knew. 'It was Pai Lian who stole my necklace, and it was she who sent you to your untimely death!' Marguerite Daisy screamed at the ghost in pure frustration. *Why is it so hard for the ghost to understand this*, she wondered?

'No, it's not true,' the ghost wailed in horror, seeds of doubt growing in her mind. Why was it so hard to think? Damn the wound on her head that was giving her pain, courtesy of the insane vagrant who had caused her death. 'My sister wouldn't do this to me!'

'Did you know Adrian was having an affair with your sister too?' Marguerite Daisy asked the ghost, turning the table to her advantage. The look of horror on the ghost's face was all she needed to confirm that the ghost wasn't even aware of that affair. Well, how could she be? The affair had been hidden so well, even from her own good self. 'I just got to know about it, if it's any consolation to you at all.'

'No . . .' the ghost wailed in denial at the betrayal, not knowing that she was the one who took her own twin sister's lover.

No one knew, neither fate nor her—it was a secret affair that no one suspected until the aftermath. 'How could she do this to me?!'

'Now, go find your sister and my husband, just leave me alone,' Marguerite Daisy said with a wicked smirk, setting the ghost on a destructive path. She never knew killing two birds with one stone would be this easy. And the best part? She didn't even have to lift a bloody finger to do it. 'Whoever you kill first, I don't really care. Just make it painful for them,' she urged.

9

16 December 1979

Lies, lies, lies . . . reeks of bloody lies,
Doesn't add up, find the connection,
Dig their graves, dig into their stories,
All with motives, beware misdirection.

Inspector Abdul Rahman sank into his plush swivel chair in his office at the Taiping Police Station as he finished reading the latest chapter that Ernest had shared, the rickety ceiling fan above him making a racket while swirling and whirling dank air around the man. The day was hot and humid right after the rain, hitting 40°C outside, a rare occurrence during monsoon season, and the Inspector was feeling more than a tad warm inside—he was hot and bothered under the collar at the pace of things, especially the Chang sisters' case. Too slow for his liking . . . like the iced lemon tea that was taking forever to be prepared. The Indian tea-lady, Shanti, must be taking her own sweet time, forgetting her boss was parched and thirsty.

'Shanti! *Mana teh limau ais saya? Kurang gula ah! Cepatlah sikit! I dah hangus ni . . .*' He shouted over the intercom asking her to get his iced lemon tea with less sugar quickly as he was burnt out. He made sure everyone heard him and knew he was in the office. It worked, everyone started picking up their pace to show they were working. Those who didn't have things to do, resorted to flashing their LLB qualification—an acronym for Look Like Busy—pretending to carry case files around as they drank their fifth cup of Americano for the day.

'Nah, here it is, Boss!' Shanti barged in with a glass of tantalizing iced lemon tea for Inspector Abdul Rahman, prepared just the way he liked it—with less sugar as the man was fat and his blood sugar was bordering on pre-diabetes. '*Minum dulu*, while it's cold,' she urged the man to drink it first.

'Call Farah, I need her to do something for me,' he told Shanti, aware that only the tea lady could find his secretary for him. Farah was always missing from her desk, preferring to hide in some corner reading trashy magazines like *My Idola*, *Love Is Here*, and *Marriage Today*, or romance novellas like *Flowers and Weddings for Me*, *Kacak & Cicak*, and *Jodoh Impian*. That girl didn't really like to be called out for her obsession with love, romance, and marriage, preferring to be seen as a God-fearing Muslimah instead.

But today, there was no need to find Farah—the girl barged into the Inspector's office directly bearing office gossips. She and Shanti were sometimes friends, sometimes enemies, but the duo was the unwitting office informants and gossipmongers; they were a veritable source of endless information and entertainment for Inspector Rahman.

'Boss, Boss . . . our front desk just booked and finger-printed Kak Tatiana Sudabasi!' Farah announced breathlessly, flailing her arms around in a dramatic fashion, almost fainting from sheer excitement. Kak Tatiana Sudabasi was a superstar from a bygone era, an actress who appeared in black-and-white movies shown over RTM. She had a few albums back then, mostly *Dondang Sayang* numbers and a few *Dangdut* hits. 'Roll out the red carpet to her cell, she just killed a drug pusher in cold blood to save her son!'

'*Sudah basilah, perempuan krepot ni*,' Shanti remarked, dismissing the poor superstar as a decrepit old hag who was as stale as yesterday's news. Who didn't know Kak Tatiana Sudabasi's son was a drug addict and squandered her fortune away? The thrice-divorced celebrity was recently seen lining up for free *bubur lambuk* at Masjid Jamek Kampung Baru!

'*Dia pun bukan angel tau, ambik wang suami untuk beri anak,*' Shanti snapped, remembering the superstar wasn't an angel either for taking her hubby's money and giving it to her child. She shook her head in frustration, wondering why some mothers spared the rod and spoilt their children, '*Lihat! Anak sudah jadi jahat macam ini,*' stressing the fact that Kak Tatiana's child had turned rogue.

Ignoring Shanti's jibes, Farah rattled on, 'The drug pusher was stabbed three times!' Without meaning to, she burst into tears, preferring to look at this murder case as a mother looking out for her son. Despite squandering away her fortune, this mother still sided with her child, her maternal instincts driving her to kill the drug pusher who got her son into drugs.

'You two are giving me a splitting headache,' Inspector Abdul Rahman groaned aloud before sipping his iced lemon tea with much relish. At least he got to cool down with this refreshing drink. Looking at Shanti and Farah who were about to bicker again, he thought he would ask them to split from his room before he lost his cool. 'Got anything else? If not, I need to look into the Chang sisters' case,' he told them curtly.

'Oh, this came for you,' Farah said and passed a copy of *The Devil's Daughter* by Audrey Kate Graves to him. Sandwiched between the pages was a dated copy of *The New York Times* with an article on Marguerite Daisy. 'There must have been a book fest this week. The author came in person and hand-delivered this just now.'

'What are you talking about?' Inspector Abdul Rahman asked Farah, ready to chastise the girl for her stupidity. Audrey Kate Graves was a renowned author and she had passed away a long time ago. This secretary of his might have mistaken someone else for the author. 'Audrey Kate Graves *sudah meninggal dunialah oii!*'

'I'm not suffering from dementia lah, Boss!' Farah explained, shaking her head in indignation. It was as clear as day that Audrey Kate Graves was there in person and handed the book to her, she swore. The author had even signed an autograph on the inside of the front cover. '*Itukan autograph dia bukan?*'

Yes, it was—right there was Audrey Kate Graves' own signature. Inspector Abdul Rahman saw it with his own eyes and felt the minute hair on his arms and neck rise. Giddy with confusion, he felt like he had been transported into *The Twilight Zone* where the lines between the reality and the supernatural were blurred.

There must be some rational explanation for this, his mind protested. Was this all Ernest's doing? He might have used his mother's signed copies to pull this prank on him. What was the significance of Marguerite Daisy's article sandwiched between the pages of Audrey Kate Graves' bestseller?

This couldn't be a prank. Ernest should know he would be a suspect in the case if he did this, trying to frame Marguerite Daisy. Why was no one suspecting Ernest Maxwell Graves in the first place? What if it was he who orchestrated all this. This unassuming fellow?

But what if he wasn't the culprit? What if this was really the ghost of Audrey Kate Graves? What did all this mean? Was she trying to protect her son?

He glanced through the article, and his heart thumped loudly, the pulse in his veins racing like the rapids in Sungai Kinabatangan. This couldn't be a coincidence, could it?

'Everybody get out!' he ordered, and as the ladies grudgingly made a beeline towards the door, he changed his mind and recalled one of them back. 'Farah you stay. I need you to call Ernest Maxwell Graves. Here's his number.'

Regret is memory in pain,
All this for a love in vain.
How heavy a price to pay,
When death claims the day.
All alone in my head,
I feel so sad, full of shame.
Even when I'm dead,
I'm still haunted by your face.
My heart was broken again,
Thinking about the life in your womb.
I went mad with the pain,
Of sending you to your tomb.

Keeping secrets, telling lies . . . that was what I did to keep my affair with Adrian Holmes hidden from everyone I loved, and to keep anyone from the press at bay. Little did I know that my lover was covertly bedding my twin sister and getting her pregnant.

'Cruelty has a human heart, and jealousy a human face,' said William Blake; and today, looking in the mirror, I could see why. I wanted to love myself more when no one else would, but I couldn't get past my reflection or the recollection of what I had done.

Did Hong Lian know I was having an affair with Adrian Holmes? Nope, no one knew. But if she did, would she leave him with a baby in her womb? Nope, no woman could.

So, I did the unthinkable, sending my beloved twin sister and her unborn child to their death at the Taiping Botanical Garden. It was a knee-jerk response! It happened so suddenly when she told me she was with Adrian's child. I didn't have time to plan her murder, so I rehashed the plots from the crime novel I had ghostwritten for him, planning to blame him for it.

'Sister, this delightful news deserves an equally wonderful gift,' I told Hong Lian upon hearing the news of her pregnancy, her happiness was killing me inside, as if she had stabbed me in the heart. 'Take this pearl necklace as my gift to you.'

If Hong Lian had an inkling of what the pearl necklace really signified, she didn't let on. I don't think many people would know of its spiritual significance these days. Pearls were so precious that ancient Chinese would put one on their loved ones' forehead to ensure a smooth journey when they passed on to the afterlife. Sometimes, the royal family would put a huge one into the mouth or under the tongue of a reigning emperor when he passed away. Here, I was putting a precious double-stranded pearl necklace onto the neck of my beloved sister to bid her goodbye forever.

'Thank you!' she enthused, eyes beaming with joy, her complexion glowing positively, thanks to the gift of life inside her womb. She didn't question how and from where I had got such a precious necklace, but if she had, I would have just fibbed on the fly that it was a piece of semi-precious jewellery I had bought with my share of royalties from the books. Well, I couldn't tell her that

I stole it from Adrian's wife during one of our trysts in his house, could I?

But what would it have mattered? Hong Lian wouldn't ever know how precious it really was. Like she could tell the difference between a diamanté and the real thing? That swine, pregnant with my lover's baby! I could feel the green-eyed monstress in me rearing its ugly head in anger.

'You should wear it when you give him the good news tonight,' I told her, faking pleasantry when deep inside too many emotions were stirring. *I . . . I had his love first, not you*, I wailed on the inside. Why us? Why were both of us twin sisters caught in this unfortunate circumstance? Life could be cruel sometimes, forcing my hand like this.

'But I can't contact him directly, not with the no-phone rule,' she cried, clutching the pearl necklace in desperation like it was her lifeline, not knowing it was more like a noose, 'Ours is not a love that can see daylight.'

Ahh . . . exactly a page off my published book—it left me open to set the trap, and the die was cast.

'But I can, sister dear. I'm his ghostwriter after all,' I reminded her, smiling to put her at ease but mentally staging the murder at a lover's haunt like it happened in my book. With a last show of affection for my sister, I planted a Judas kiss on her forehead, 'I'll tell him to meet you at the Taiping Botanical Garden at midnight, if it's okay with you.'

How I wish you could see,
How broken my heart is,
Breaking in my soul,
Falling down to hell,

Like a drop of tear,
Filled with sins.
What heart?
Do I even deserve one?
And now,
I no longer have one.

10

The White Lotus ghost clenched her fists to control her heart-wrenching scream, her ethereal body shaking. She had to get hold of herself before her self-hatred, grief, and guilt got the better of her. She stopped typing for a moment and started sobbing, crying her heart out.

'Oh, Adrian, look what you had me do,' the ghost said to herself, terribly conflicted inside, unsure of what was right and wrong anymore, torn on all sides. She had wanted to expose her lover's heinous wrongdoings to her twin sister, but things took a different turn. 'How did this turn from a hatchet job into a confessional piece?'

Was it guilt? Was it love? she asked herself, a little angry at the sudden change of direction that made everything go awry. Maybe it was madness!

With a sad look, the White Lotus ghost turned to see Ernest sleeping on his bed with his back turned to her and noticed the blanket had slipped off. *Oh dear! This man needs a mother to pick up after him, can't seem to do anything right,* she thought pitifully. Worried that he might catch a cold, she flew by his bedside to cover him up with the blanket.

'What would you think of me in the morning when you read my manuscript?' she whispered softly and thought Ernest was a lucky man not to have fallen in love yet. 'Don't fall in love, don't lose your heart, mind, and soul like I did,' she cautioned him, this time whispering in his ears.

Don't think unkindly of me please, she begged silently in her heart, *I came when the pain was unbearable, I had to do what I did because of love.* Love makes people do crazy things, even now when she had to make a 180-degree turn, not that Ernest or the world would understand her extenuating circumstances. 'Oh, what would you do for love?' She asked no one in particular; she gave up everything for love even when she was already dead with nothing more to give.

As the White Lotus ghost turned away from Ernest, she noticed something out of the ordinary. The colour on her cheeks turned a bright red when she saw what he had put under her chair by the table—a ceremonial bowl of uncooked rice grains with a raw egg on top and a single chopstick stuck straight in the middle like a tombstone—clearly meant for the dead as the Chinese usually put these things under the bed of the dead or under the coffin during a wake as part of the funeral customs.

How the hell did I miss it when I came in? she wondered. It spooked her a little since it reminded her of her own mortality— although she was very much a ghost now. The offering was part of a tradition to prevent any lingering hunger in the afterlife . . . clearly meant for her.

Oh, don't tell me about hunger, you idiot, the ghost mentally reproached at Ernest, *you don't know what I'm hungry for.* She couldn't help feeling a little insulted inside, and dashed away through the wall, disappearing in a huff. In her wake, the wind blew the blanket off a very shocked and shivering Ernest.

11

Achoo . . . Ernest Maxwell Graves sneezed in front of Inspector Abdul Rahman who backed away like the writer had an infectious disease or something. He had woken up shivering, and having received the call from the Inspector's office, had rushed to see him.

'Caught a cold?' the Inspector asked with an arched eyebrow, his fingers drumming his desk in anticipation of Ernest's reply, 'Wear more clothes at night, it's monsoon season now.'

'It's probably nothing,' Ernest said, dismissing the Inspector's concern while seated in the latter's cramped corner office, going through the photocopies of Pai Lian's latest chapters. 'I'll grab a Panadol later to be sure,' he assured the Inspector.

There were more pressing matters than catching a cold right now. They had thought the cold-blooded murder was a straightforward case—a famous crime novelist took a page out of his books to commit a crime by getting his pregnant mistress killed before his jealous wife could find out about his affair. Everything was going by the book until this latest confessional chapter by Pai Lian brought an unexpected twist.

'Do we release Adrian Holmes?' Ernest asked the Inspector, a little lost about what to do next. Based on Pai Lian's confessional chapter, she had exonerated Adrian Holmes from all blame. With the homeless vagrant still at large, it looked like Adrian Holmes would get away scot-free after all. 'You can't hold a man if he is innocent,' Ernest reminded an agitated Inspector Rahman.

'I really thought we had it in the bag already, I really did. Damn it!' the Inspector snapped and drew down the blinds of his office abruptly in case there were any prying eyes in the police station. He hated sudden surprises and detested people throwing a spanner in the works, especially someone who got him to incarcerate Adrian Holmes in the first place. Didn't Pai Lian give him the novel she had ghostwritten with all the parallels and evidences? Now why was she throwing in this unexpected twist . . . that she in fact was the reason why her twin sister was dead?!

Ernest was not loving this either. The plot twist was sending chills down his spine. Was he really in the room with a psychotic ghost present? What if she harmed him? But if she had wanted him dead, she would have left him to die the first time, no? He shook his head, not knowing what to think anymore.

'Let's go through the facts again, in case we missed something,' Ernest said with a troubled sigh.

'We have everything to persecute Adrian Holmes,' the Inspector declared as he sat into his chair and sipped his *teh tarik*, 'that idiot committed murder by the book, his book . . . exactly as per *A Bridge to Murderville*.'

'A book that had been ghostwritten by Pai Lian,' Ernest added, scratching his head and trying to piece the story together again to make a coherent case file. 'It must also be noted that Pai Lian has strong motives for revenge.'

'Ya, imagine having an affair with the crime novelist, only to find out that the bastard had bedded and impregnated her twin,' the Inspector recalled, shaking his head in disbelief, 'That's criminal! How not to feel hurt by this?! If I were Pai Lian, I'd shoot him like the toad he is!'

'So, did Pai Lian really send her twin to her death?' Ernest asked the Inspector, pausing to hear what the rotund man had to say. It was plausible that in a fit of anger, Pai Lian had done just that, using the pearl necklace as bait to draw a borrowed knife—tempting the deranged vagrant to do the deed, the vagrant subsequently taking the blame! 'So, is this why Pai Lian committed suicide? Out of regret for causing the death of her own twin sister?'

A series of urgent knocks was heard on the door that brought their conversation to a halt. Before Inspector Abdul Rahman could give the permission to enter, both the Malay secretary and the Indian tea-lady barged in excitedly. *What now?* The Inspector thought irritably, *buat kacau saje* these two jokers.

'What do you want now, Farah?' he asked the Malay secretary before turning his attention to the Indian tea-lady, 'Ahh . . . good that you are here, Shanti. Get me another glass of *teh tarik*. Our guest would like another cup of Milo Dinosaur.'

'Boss, boss . . . *tengok*!' Farah said excitedly while pushing her mobile phone into the Inspector's hands and showing him the clip of the ghost in a white robe, '*Our jail ada hantu berjubah putih!*' Without batting an eyelid, she quickly took the chance to introduce herself to Ernest before her boss could shoo her out of his room, 'Hi, my name is Farah, but you can call me your *dinda!*'

'Hi, Farah,' Ernest said, feeling a tad awkward that his good looks had caught the secretary's eyes although he didn't quite catch what *dinda* meant. What she said next before walking out of the room, got him startled, 'We got your mother's signed copy of *The Devil's Daughter.*'

'Oh, about that, swear to me that you didn't have anything to do with it!' the Inspector said to Ernest. Looking at the man up and down to check for telltale signs, he told a shocked Ernest, 'Farah claims that your mother had come in person to deliver a signed copy of her book.'

Jealous that Farah had gotten all the attention, Shanti, the tea lady, downplayed her frenemy's glory by saying to Ernest, 'Don't pay no heed to Farah, *dia sikit kooky*. You *ingat ini Twilight Zone ah?* She probably bought a signed copy from eBay *lah!*' In a huff, she stormed away and slammed the door shut.

'What was that about? I swear I didn't have anything to do with it!' Ernest declared his innocence to the inspector. Did his beloved mother really come from beyond? He would like to think so even though it was probably what Shanti had said . . . that Farah had done this as a prank to get his attention.

'Never mind that if you've nothing to do with it,' the Inspector told him, loathing to explain what would appear a prank when there was something more important to discuss. 'Look at this video that has been going viral, taken by one of our night guards. Apparently, Pai Lian had visited Adrian Holmes in the prison.'

'Oh, I wonder what they have been talking about,' Ernest remarked as he scrutinized the video.

The image of Adrian and a lady in white was grainy and their conversation couldn't be heard as the audio was almost non-existent. 'Hmm . . . is this why she had a change of heart? She fell for his words again?!'

'We don't know for sure since there's no sound,' Inspector Abdul Rahman admitted, but he had his suspicions. This Pai Lian could be a fool in love, even after her death. She might be trying to spring her lover free despite what he had done to her twin sister. 'This would really explain why the plot had taken a surprising turn.'

Remembering his dream, Ernest recalled Hong Lian's words, *Blood is on her hands. Here I was thinking blood is thicker than water.* Was Pai Lian complicit in her twin sister's murder? Or that Hong Lian was angry at her sister for the change of heart in avenging her?

'How true is Pai Lian's confessional manuscript anyway?' a tired Ernest contemplated aloud, wondering if it was to be believed at all. How could anyone take a ghost's word for it? What if this ghost had an agenda? What if they unwittingly fell prey to Pai Lian's ulterior motives?

'Who can really tell? Where's the proof?' he asked the Inspector, feeling a massive headache erupting in his head, 'In a court of law, facts talk and bullshit walks.'

'If we talk facts, there's more to this story then,' Inspector Abdul Rahman opined, drumming his fingers on his table while ruminating on the possibilities, 'We have not explored the other suspects with motives, you know.'

'Who?' a surprised Ernest asked, his eyes widening in shock, not aware of another suspect in the picture, 'Who else has the motive?'

'Marguerite Daisy Holmes,' the Inspector said, a little amused that Ernest hadn't suspected Adrian Holmes' wife at all. This woman was just waiting to get her hands on her husband's riches, probably fed-up already with his philandering ways, and wanted to take her revenge on him and his mistresses once and for all.

'I've done some digging into her past. She was an actress at one time, very adept at playing victims,' he continued to postulate while dropping the copy of *The New York Times*— the one purportedly left by Audrey Kate Graves—onto the table for Ernest to read; its headline displayed prominently: MARGUERITE DAISY VINDICATED: WINS $100 MILLION FORTUNE FROM LATE FASHION MOGUL.

'She had buried a previous husband who is now pushing daisies from six feet under,' he told Ernest with a knowing smile, pleased that he had unearthed another shocking piece of crucial information, 'Surprises don't really end, do they?'

12

'I make no bones about hating mistresses,' a defiant Marguerite Daisy Holmes declared to Lady Nightshade as she helped the psychic medium onto her expensive velvet chaise lounge from the bespoke London-based designer Sebastian Cox. 'Or the fact that I have a bone to pick with the husbands who keep them.'

'Men will be men, can't keep their boners in check,' Lady Nightshade remarked sarcastically as she grimaced in pain after a trip to the chiropractor for her misaligned bones, a nasty result from the fiasco with the Red Lotus ghost some three nights ago.

Her recuperation at the luxurious home of Marguerite Daisy was sorely needed but if her condition worsened, she would have to see the Chinese chiropractor *sinseh* or a *tit-tar* bone-setting master by the name of Kim Wang in Istana Larut, Taiping, which she would hate—she didn't relish smelling like a sulphurous swamp for weeks on end. The last time she had her bones realigned by the *tit-tar* master, she peed torrents into her pants, an embarrassment she wouldn't like repeating anytime soon. 'You've said you wanted a tarot card reading, dear? Pass me my cards please,' she said to Marguerite.

'There you go,' Marguerite Daisy handed over the tarot deck to Lady Nightshade. It was a very precious Visconti-Sforza set that was reputedly hand-painted with oil paint, gold, and silver on heavy paper by Bonifacio Bembo in Italy back in 1425.

'You should shuffle the deck my dear, it has to be done by the querent,' Lady Nightshade reminded Marguerite Daisy, and said, 'Concentrate on your questions, send your intent to the universe, delve deeply into your subconscious.'

Feeling ready after shuffling, Marguerite Daisy passed the deck to Lady Nightshade who proceeded with cards' placement on the table using the Celtic cross tarot spread. This kind of formation would enable the psychic medium to see the overall big picture of the situation at hand, taking into account the present, challenges, subconscious, past, future, near future, internal and external influences, as well as hopes and fears—with the last card indicating the outcome of the querent's question.

'Oh . . . how very interesting,' Lady Nightshade remarked and sighed as she read the first card indicating the present—*The Tower*—which meant upheaval, broken pride, and disaster. 'Your house is in shambles, my dear. Your pride is bruised and there is disaster.'

'That's true, tell me something I don't know,' Marguerite Daisy admitted bluntly, knowing it was an understatement to say the least. Disaster indeed; her husband was in prison and he was about to write her off from his will. *Nope, not going to happen*, she swore to herself. 'What did the second card say?'

'Hmm . . . the second card indicates challenges, and it's *The Lovers* . . . in reverse, oh dear,' Lady Nightshade told Marguerite, shaking her head with a sigh. With it in reverse, it could only mean that there was a loss of balance in her love life, one sidedness and disharmony. 'You face challenges from your husband's mistresses, it would seem.'

'Well, we know who his whores are,' Marguerite Daisy snapped bitterly. Alive, they were her husband's mistresses. Dead, they were her ghosts to contend with. 'I'll deal with them. I've sown discord between the twin sisters and set the Red Lotus ghost on a deadly rampage.'

'The third card indicates your subconscious mind,' Lady Nightshade revealed as she slowly upturned it to see *The Chariot*, which indicated direction, control, and will power. 'Ahh . . . you had set something in motion. You didn't stay a victim for long, did you?'

'I always play a victim on screen, never in real life,' Marguerite Daisy said, proud of the fact that she could separate reel life from real life. If only this psychic medium knew what she did to set things in motion, the latter would pack up her bags and take the next flight home, back to New Orleans, in a heartbeat.

Well, wasn't she the one who had left her pearl necklace under her bed for the mistress to find out? Why did no one wonder why such a precious piece of jewellery wasn't kept in a bank vault? Or the fact that she didn't bother to check under the bed the other time? All of this drama required great acting, not that the Academy Awards committee would know about it.

'You've got everything right so far,' Marguerite Daisy said, appreciative of the fact that this Lady Nightshade was a bona fide psychic medium, not a cent was wasted in hiring her. But there was more that Marguerite Daisy needed to know and she asked, 'What is the fourth card?'

'Well, well, well . . . it is *The Emperor* . . . in reverse,' Lady Nightshade told Marguerite Daisy. The fourth card revealed the past and in its reversed state, it indicated tyranny, rigidity, and coldness. 'An ex-husband perhaps?'

'*Ex* is the operative word,' Marguerite Daisy replied with a sly smile, knowing this tyrant had been dealt with and that she had acquired the fashion mogul's vast fortune, way before her marriage to Adrian Holmes. Well, served him right for putting her in cold storage after finding mistresses from the runways of Paris, London, and New York. 'Well, what does the fifth card say?'

'The fifth card is the far future card, and it is *The Wheel of Fortune*,' Lady Nightshade said, recalling what it really meant—change, cycle, inevitable fate. 'Looks like you are destined to inherit Adrian Holmes' fortune after all, my dear.'

'Oh great, some good news at last,' a beaming Marguerite Daisy said and breathed a sigh of relief. It looked like great wealth was on the cards for her. *Goodbye, Adrian Holmes. May you rot in hell with your whores,* Marguerite Daisy cursed him in her mind. 'What about the sixth card? It's the near future card, isn't it?' she asked.

'Yes, it is indeed,' Lady Nightshade said to her, and upturned the sixth card only to find it was *The Hanged Man*, which meant sacrifices and martyrdom were on the way. What did this mean? That Adrian Holmes would be hanged? What was this martyrdom about? Who would make the sacrifices? White Lotus or Red Lotus? Or perhaps it was someone else, the cards didn't really say as they relied on the reader and the querent's intuition to decipher.

'Someone is going to die,' Marguerite Daisy assumed. Let's hope it was the no-good husband of hers so she could inherit all his money. The ghosts could fight amongst themselves to play the martyr, for all she cared. 'The seventh card? What does it say?'

'The seventh card reveals internal influences,' Lady Nightshade pre-empted Marguerite Daisy. It turned out to be *The High Priestess*, which denotes intuition and inner voice. Well, there was no surprise there. 'Looks like I will be your high priestess for a while, it says.'

'Yes, that goes without saying,' Marguerite Daisy said, thankful for Lady Nightshade's help with the mystical insights, an advantage badly needed because she was battling not just any nemeses but supernatural beings like the two ghosts. 'I can't do this without you, so stick around and we will prevail,' she told Lady Nightshade who nodded in agreement.

'The eighth card is the external influences card,' Lady Nightshade explained to Marguerite Daisy. As it turned out, it was *The Empress* that symbolized motherhood, fertility, and nature, which perplexed the psychic medium for a bit, 'Eh, how come your mother is involved in this?'

That revelation shook Marguerite Daisy a little. *More than you would ever know, less than I cared to let you know*, Marguerite Daisy quipped to herself, vowing to take the secret to her grave.

Way before Lady Nightshade, Marguerite Daisy had sought the help of other psychic mediums to contact her mother, Petunia Yates, from beyond the grave and that old woman was most obliging in assisting her daughter to rectify the latter's marriage woes—usually by getting rid of bad husbands. Why should this time be any different?

'Well, we did contact my mother during the seance, right?' Marguerite Daisy replied coolly to Lady Nightshade, reminding the psychic medium of their most unfortunate encounter with the Red Lotus ghost, 'Remember that other day?'

There was an uncomfortable silence and Lady Nightshade bit her tongue before any word could roll out of it. *Marguerite Daisy is hiding secrets, big ones, too*, she thought, but she would let this slide lest she unwittingly aggravated this rich benefactor and lost her handsome fee—money that would come to good use, she was sure.

'The ninth card reads your hopes and fears,' Lady Nightshade continued with her tarot reading, and saw it was *The Justice*, which represented cause and effect, clarity, and truth.

'You hope for justice served and fear the consequences. What have you done?' she asked Marguerite Daisy who fidgeted in her seat.

'Oh, never you mind,' Marguerite Daisy brushed off Lady Nightshade's query, afraid she might let on too much if she weren't careful. It won't do her any good if this psychic medium knew more than she should. This tarot reading session was uncannily accurate she felt, and what remained now was the last card. She was almost too afraid to find out. 'What's the outcome? It is the last card, isn't it?' she asked anxiously, changing the subject ever so subtly and was dying inside to know what it was.

'Why yes, you are correct Marguerite Daisy,' Lady Nightshade said, ignoring the fact that her benefactor was deflecting her question to avoid answering it. *Ahh . . . so many secrets this one*, the psychic medium surmised with a smile, *and her mother, too—so many skeletons in the closet!*

'Here's the last one,' the psychic medium declared while turning the outcome card up—it was *Death*, a picture of fatality represented by a human skeleton. It meant an end of a cycle, a finality! *Ahh . . . skeleton again, the universe is saying something. An end, but for whom?*

'No . . .' Marguerite Daisy screamed, hating her outcome card and swept the tarot spread off from the table in an outburst of fury—even though she knew in her heart that it didn't mean death per se, just an ending for a new beginning. 'I . . . It cannot end this way!' she shrieked and burst into angry tears, 'I won't let it, I won't!'

13

Night of the murder, 1 November 1979

Beautiful by day, desolate by night—that was the lake in Taiping Botanical Garden as seen through the eyes of a homeless vagrant with a fractured mind . . . on the night of the murder in November 1979. In his head lost to delusions, he had mindlessly robbed and killed a beautiful Chinese girl in red with a double-stranded pearl necklace around her neck.

'The pearls called to me,' the homeless vagrant had told the police when he was interrogated, feeling no remorse as he recounted what he did to Chang Hong Lian, the victim—stabbing her right in the heart and dumping her body into the lake. Little did he know that the victim had also fractured her skull on hitting a stone beneath the lake, which would have made it impossible for her to think straight, dead or alive. The voices had told him to do it, the poor vagrant kept claiming to the police, 'Come kill me, the pearls had said.'

'You'll love what Fair Petunia would do; Wins your heart and kisses all night,' the homeless vagrant suddenly broke into a song-and-dance skit, singing the 1925-oldie, 'Fair Petunia' by Dahlia Brown, much to the surprise of the policemen around him who had dismissed him as an illiterate loony. 'Love, love, love, my Fair Petunia, the only thing I love; Fair Petunia will send me to my grave.'

'Come on, old man, we'll send you to the loony bin in Taiping Hospital,' a policeman said to the homeless vagrant while taking a dig at the latter's 'looney tune' skit. His colleague, a diver, had retrieved the murder weapon from the lake—a rusty old dagger that had to be sent to the forensic department for analysis, not that it would do any good since it had corroded and had been under water for some time already. 'We're done for the night people. This Grammy winner has admitted to the killing, and we have the murder weapon already. Let's go, I'm going to be late for *Malam Jumaat dengan bini I*,' the policeman told his friend, eager to spend the holy Friday night with his wifey.

'In here?' the homeless vagrant asked suspiciously as he entered handcuffed into the police van, which was 'affectionately' called Black Maria by those in the force and the press. He took his seat by the elegant, well-preserved English lady dressed in a Chantilly lace gown, carrying an exquisite brolly with an ivory handle that was carved with petunia blooms. She smiled at him and made a zipping motion across her lips to urge him to keep quiet but the loony man in his ignorance asked aloud, '*Lu siapa? Pergi hi-tea eh?*—essentially asking the mysterious woman who she was and if she was going for hi-tea.

'Who is he talking to? *Sewel betul otai ni kan?*' the policeman remarked to his diver friend, dismissing the old-timer detainee as someone not in the right mind. His friend couldn't care less what the crazy vagrant was up to, saying, '*Otak dah tak center!*'—pegging the half-wit as an unhinged weirdo that he was.

None of them could see the English lady at the back of the van with the homeless vagrant when the doors were slammed shut. For if they did, they would be spooked and would have turned their eyes away. *It is better this way*, the English lady thought, *no one will see their tears and not a soul will hear their screams when the moment comes to end their lives forever.*

'Your wife got new perfume, ah?' the diver asked the policeman suddenly, thinking her scent had rubbed off on the man. There was a strange floral scent in the air, and he couldn't quite make out what it was. 'It is getting stronger by the minute. You better advise her not to put so much of it. Too overpowering!'

'Strange that you mentioned it,' the policeman replied, thinking it was his diver friend who was the source of this heavy scent. He had wanted to mention it earlier, but then thought he shouldn't, lest he be misunderstood. Not all men liked to be called out for wearing a feminine perfume when they should be wearing cologne, especially a petunia-scented one at that. 'I thought you took up a hobby growing petunias,' he jested dryly, trying to be diplomatic, as best as he could under this circumstance.

'I didn't,' the diver told his friend, but as tradition and culture dictated, they were supposed to make *no* mention of it or acknowledge it even, especially in the dead of the night. Scary stories of Pontianak and sweet frangipani fragrance came to mind. This might not smell like the feared bloom, but it stood to reason they be cautious as well, lest it be the harbinger of misfortune and death. It wasn't long before goosebumps prickled their skin and their hair stood on ends. 'Let's get out of here quickly,' the diver urged as his policeman friend hopped onto the driver's seat to speed away.

No words or frivolous banter were exchanged during the entire drive except when their Black Maria suddenly encountered a blocked road in the middle of nowhere, the cause—a fallen raintree too heavy to move without tractors. *Oh great, just what we needed*, the men moaned and complained mentally, still afraid to make a sound.

It necessitated a detour via the old road adjacent to the trunk road, and seeing there was no other option in sight, they reluctantly made the turn into a dusty dirt lane without streetlamps. Immediately, they regretted it as the night mist turned into rolling fog, blurring their vision and slowing down their vehicle.

Macam ini mati le kita semua, the men thought, knowing they were in dire straits and their misfortune wouldn't end well. To make matters worse, the crazy homeless vagrant in the back of the van started singing that 'Fair Petunia' song again.

If I could dance like a singing star,
Up on a stage I call Fair Petunia back,
I'm crazy about my Fair Petunia, the only one I love,

Fair, fair, fair Petunia the only one I love,
Fair Petunia is sending me home to my grave.

Horror of horrors, a local idiot singing an old classic from the
twenties no less, unheard of in this part of the world. The officers
of the force were just starting to realize something was terribly
wrong, an omen they didn't quite pick up when that crazy vagrant
first started singing.

Not losing a moment, the policeman stopped driving and
beckoned his diver partner to get down. They opened the doors
to see the vagrant alone, oblivious to the presence of the English
lady already standing behind them.

'I always loved American classics when I was alive, even as a
little girl growing up in London,' the English lady confessed in her
heavy British accent, startling both men who were at their wits'
end. 'Oh, how rude of me for not introducing myself properly,
I am Madam Petunia Yates, if you haven't already guessed.'

. 'Who the hell?!' both men sputtered simultaneously, unaware
that she was Marguerite Daisy Holmes' late mother. 'Where did
you come from, lady? Back off!'

Her sudden appearance had undoubtedly spooked them, and
judging by what she had said, it was clear that she was a ghost.
When I was alive, they heard her saying clearly.

'Language, gentlemen!' Madam Petunia Yates cautioned the
officers with mock indignation when she heard the four-letter
word 'hell'. They were in the presence of a true lady of high
station, for goodness' sake!

'Where have you come from?' the diver asked.

'Well, if you must know, I hitched a ride here via those
precious pearls, all the way from the other side!'

Her daughter, Marguerite Daisy, needed her . . . again. A loving
mother would always be there for her child, and hers transcended
beyond death, thanks to the help of psychic mediums.

Initially, Marguerite Daisy had left the precious pearl necklace
under the bed for the mistress to find, so her mother could exact

revenge on her behalf. Who knew this Pai Lian would give it away to her unwitting twin sister, Hong Lian, upon learning of her pregnancy. One thing led to another, and now, here they were . . . cutting loose ends.

'All of you must die,' Madam Petunia Yates told them with a look of mock regret on her face; secretly relishing her moment to let loose with her supernatural powers that she had accrued as a witch when she was alive. 'Be a dear and die screaming for me, will you?' she taunted the men.

'Threatening the officers of the law? Eat lead, lady!' The angry policeman fired rapid shots at Madam Petunia Yates who deflected them with her opened brolly—an enchanted tool of dark magic, enhanced by the ivory handle made from the tusk of a boar demon.

'W . . . What?' the bewildered policeman exclaimed when he realized all his efforts were in vain.

'Temper, temper . . .' Madam Petunia Yates hummed the Mary Poppins song as her opened brolly hoisted her up into the air like a spectre of doom. From the menacing height above, she pointed her perfectly manicured index finger at the policeman and a lightning streak from the dark sky blasted the poor man into an incendiary mess.

'No, no, no . . .' the diver-friend yelled in horror as he made a dash into the Black Maria for safety. Unfortunately, for him and the vagrant, Madam Petunia Yates closed her brolly and used it as a giant wand to raise a cyclone that overturned the van and rolled it violently across the dirt road. Seeing the vehicle turned turtle and satisfied that no one could survive her assault, Madam Petunia Yates subsequently disappeared from this plane of existence.

As fate would have it, one man did survive the ordeal—the homeless, crazy vagrant. Injured and in pain, he mindlessly walked away from the site and headed to the only place close enough for him to call home . . . The Taiping Botanical Garden.

14

Going home, going home, I'm just going home, the vagrant sang the funeral song that came out of nowhere in his mind, *Quiet-like slip away, I'll be going home*. Then his madness set in, driving his tongue to sing it with other words, *The moon lights the way, restless sins all done; Shadows come, death of day, hell has just begun.*

Like a salmon swimming upriver to spawn and die, the vagrant walked 'home' to the lake and waited to die. At Taiping Botanical Garden, he knew his time was up. His dream might have been over, but his nightmare had just started. After all, he did the crime, it was time to pay the ferry man his dime. Not that he had any coin, if truth be told.

'Where is the ferry man?' the vagrant asked impatiently as he listened to the cicadas for an answer—he got none. Feeling that he had to pee, he walked to a nearby raintree to answer nature's call. Before he relieved himself, he had the presence of mind to ask permission from a Datuk Kong deity to pee onto the latter's domain. Failure to do so would result in severe repercussions, it was believed—he could be cursed with testicular swelling, *not something anyone would want on their way to hell*, he thought to himself.

'Datuk Kong, Datuk Kong, *tumpang kencing*,' the vagrant pleaded as he unleashed a torrent of pee, '*Terima kasih*, Datuk Kong.'

Having done his business, he zipped up and turned around, only to be freaked out—he almost peed his pants again. Standing in front of him was a *Zhizha* bamboo-and-paper effigy of the dead, typically present during Chinese funeral rites. It was crafted wearing a glorious female Chinese opera costume, its painted face smiling inanely, its eyes vacant and soulless without any life in them.

'Sorry, I not Chinese,' the vagrant muttered incoherently, knowing very well what this was all about. Even though he was multiracial, he had seen enough of this having been born, raised, and now, very likely, would die in Perak.

Bamboo-and-paper creations represented offerings to the dead by the living, from what he heard and knew, to be burnt on the last day of the funeral to accompany the deceased in their afterlife. And in his life thus far, he had seen so many types of paper offerings—from cars to clothes, and houses to currency notes.

The Chinese opera effigy started moving—first slowly, then faster—dancing to an imaginary *minzu yuetuan*, Chinese funeral orchestra, that was accompanied by the piercing wail of *suona* double-reed instrument alongside brass gongs, flower drums, and *sheng* mouth organs.

Swirling effortlessly with acrobatic moves, the effigy staged a *Jingju* opera performance akin to a live show that the Chinese would put up during the Hungry Ghost Festival to entertain the spirits—only this time it was the other way around with the dead staging one for the living, or in the vagrant's case, a soon-to-be-dead person.

'Sit here?' the vagrant asked as he was escorted by another two servant effigies that came out of nowhere to usher him to a front-row seat reserved for honoured guests; only this time, it was reserved for the living instead of the dead.

'Wah, so many people,' the vagrant remarked in passing when he turned around to look at the other attendees watching the opera, completely unaware that those were all spirits with him being the only one still human. '*Banyak bagus*,' he murmured, thinking everything was mighty good and fine.

Then, without so much as a warning, the Chinese opera took a more dramatic turn as the woman effigy effortlessly somersaulted backwards doing impossible back flips while more *Zhizha* effigies in glorious paper costumes came into view, unveiling a paper-and-bamboo mansion rising steadily from the lake, unstained by its water and flanked by the water lilies.

In a scene straight from a horrifying nightmare, the mansion's reflection projected a different reality with it burning in hell and lost souls screaming in agony.

'My sister, Pai Lian, had given me a glorious funeral with a wealth of paper offerings before her suicide,' Hong Lian declared to the vagrant as she sauntered out of the mansion, her arms cradling a bouquet of eighteen red lotuses, 'Blessings I intend to turn into curses to deal with her and those who have wronged me, starting with you.'

The vagrant looked at his victim and cried with happiness, welcoming his pain to assuage his guilt. He knew he deserved every bit of torment coming his way for his sins, and couldn't wait for his final release, away from this life of suffering and the cruel, cruel world. *Anything is better than living like this*, he thought to himself, crying shamelessly like a mindless idiot waiting for rapture.

'Behold, the first level of hell,' Hong Lian said and threw the first stalk of red lotuses at the hapless vagrant, initiating a scene from hell staged by the cast of paper effigies—The Hell of Tongue-Ripping. 'Confess your lies and cruel words, so all hell can hear what you did,' she screamed at him maniacally without mercy.

Not bothering with his reply, bailiff effigies grabbed the vagrant by the arms and hair and pulled out his tongue with a tong while a demon effigy sliced it with a sharp knife. 'Owwww . . .' the vagrant screamed in pain as blood spurted out from his wound.

'Now, the second level of hell, you won't ask for seconds,' Hong Lian sneered wickedly while throwing the second stalk of red lotuses at the vagrant. Ten-hand maiden effigies with scissors danced in circles around the victim before overwhelming him, pulling at his hands to cut all his fingers off one by one—each more painful than the other, making the vagrant scream louder and louder. 'Argh . . .' was all he could manage to yell, but in vain.

Not done with the torture yet, Hong Lian threw the third stalk of red lotuses to signify the start of the third level of hell. On the ground where the lotuses fell, a paper tree grew in its place—complete with sharp knives. 'Feel the pain when you sow discord,' Hong Lian said, 'At the third level of hell with the knife trees!'

On cue, the vagrant was dragged to be hung on the tree of knives by ghoulish grey effigies where the branches armed with knives slashed at him. 'No . . .' he protested as ribbons of flesh fell from his bones.

'Don't die now, you need to suffer more at the fourth level of hell,' Hong Lian said as she dropped another stalk of lotuses at the vagrant's feet, 'Reflect at the Mirrors of Retribution.'

To the vagrant's horror, skeleton effigies came forth and held up paper mirrors lined with reflective silver foil to show his crimes. In them, he saw all his crimes; the truth of what he did was more painful than the lies he had told himself.

Just kill me and be done with it, the vagrant thought since he couldn't talk. His guilt grew as heavy as his sins and it broke the mirrors—the damage mysteriously reflected onto his body, shattering his bones and flesh like glass.

'Now, it's the fifth level of hell,' Hong Lian announced as she watched her green demonic effigies dragging the pieces of the vagrant's bones and flesh to be dumped into the lake, 'The Hell of Steamers.'

Even when shattered into bodily pieces, the vagrant could still feel the excruciating pain of rising temperatures from the lake, boiling and steaming his soul like hell had no mercy. As though his torment wasn't enough, his pieces of bones and flesh were dragged from the lake—its water now calm and serene as before—to be prepared for the next stage of torture.

'You will now suffer the sixth level of hell,' Hong Lian said and threw the sixth stalk of red lotuses on the ground where it grew into a metal pillar, 'The Hell of Copper Pillars.'

Here was where the hellish purple effigies chained back the vagrant's bodily pieces onto a copper pillar that was growing hotter by the second. Fully formed again, his sad face was a picture of seared flesh with a big gaping mouth that emitted no sound—verily in hell no one could hear him scream.

'Now, you suffer the seventh level of hell,' Hong Lian told the vagrant as she threw down the seventh stalk of red lotuses that exploded into a heap of sharp blades that kept multiplying, 'The Hell of the Mountain of Knives.'

Before the vagrant had a moment's respite, he was chained onto meat hooks by flying bird-like demon effigies to be dragged up the mountain of knives, a heinous torture that reopened his wounds with fresh cuts to his body and caused him much suffering.

'At the height of the pile, you now suffer the eighth level of hell,' Hong Lian said to the traumatized victim, as she threw the eighth stalk of red lotuses into the air and they floated to the vagrant, 'The Hell of Ice Mountain.'

Upon touching him, the red lotuses sent chills down his spine while sharp ice crystals burst all over his body, freezing the vagrant into an ice sculpture in an instant. As if suffering from frostbite wasn't enough, the poor man could feel the cold right down to his soul.

'We're halfway done, you're now at the ninth level of hell—The Hell of Cauldrons of Oil.' Hong Lian reminded her victim, relishing the torture she was inflicting upon her murderer.

The blades melted into a cauldron with the vagrant still inside as ghostly white effigies poured vats of oil onto the victim—essentially frying him alive while ignoring his screams.

'Brace yourself, now is the tenth level of hell,' Hong Lian said as she kissed the tenth stalk of red lotuses like a matador and threw it into the cauldron, which expanded to form a bull ring: 'The Hell of Cattle Pit.'

Cattle effigies created an earth-shattering stampede and gored the vagrant, flinging his body up with their horns and crushing his body down with their hooves, leaving a bloody mess.

'No rest for the wicked, it's time for the eleventh level of hell,' Hong Lian declared as she danced to the flower drum song before throwing the eleventh stalk of red lotuses onto the bloody mess that mysteriously reformed the vagrant to suffer another round of torture, 'The Hell of Crushing Boulders.'

Boulders the size of asteroids fell from the skies as the vagrant ran helter-skelter looking for cover. But it was to no avail as he was crushed by an asteroid as big as a car. Body broken beyond recognition, he could only plead for mercy with his eyes and tears.

'Don't expect mercy from me when you showed me none,' Hong Lian told her murderer bluntly. 'Next, we have the twelfth level of hell—the Hell of Mortars and Pestles.'

By the time the twelfth stalk of red lotuses touched the victim to reform him, the boulder had morphed into a mortar and pestle. They were worse than the stationary boulders because the mortar and pestle actively moved on their own volition to crush the vagrant with immense force again and again till he was nothing but a pile of pulp.

'The thirteenth level of hell awaits,' Hong Lian announced gleefully as red double-headed mutant effigies dragged the bloody remains of the poor vagrant into the lake, 'The Hell of Blood Pool.'

As her thirteenth stalk of red lotuses touched the victim, he reformed in the pool only to find its water turning red with blood beasts swimming around him. Terrified, he tried to swim to the shore but one of the beasts caught him, dragging and submerging him in the depth of their pool while sucking all his blood.

'Die and die again, you certainly deserve your fate,' Hong Lian spat in hatred and anger, 'the fourteenth level of hell starts now— The Hell of Wrongful Dead.'

The vagrant hadn't just killed her but her unborn child in her womb as well. As punishment, he was reformed again by the virtue of the fourteenth lotus stalk only to find paper effigies of babies crawling out of the dirt and crying to heaven for justice. In response, the heaven shed rain of pain that bore deeply into the vagrant's body like acid eating into flesh while winds of sorrow pelted his wounds with sands most mercilessly.

'Children, let's start the fifteenth level of hell,' Hong Lian cajoled the babies and threw down the gauntlet with her fifteenth stalk of red lotuses, 'The Hell of Dismemberment.'

In retaliation, the babies grew razor-sharp teeth and claws and crawled their way to the vagrant, overwhelming him with their sheer number and tearing him to pieces. There was nowhere to run, everywhere were babies crying out for vengeance.

'The sixteenth level of hell is now yours to suffer,' Hong Lian said and threw another stalk of red lotuses down, just as the lotuses in the lake, all burst into flames, 'The Hell of the Mountain of Fire.'

From the corner of his eyes, the vagrant saw the sixteenth red lotuses start burning and its fire spreading to the baby effigies—burning him along with it. They all screamed in terror and agony.

'Reform to suffer the seventeenth level of hell,' Hong Lian commanded and threw another stalk of red lotuses to revive him, 'The Hell of Mills'—a fitting punishment for those who oppressed the weak.

Hordes of farmer effigies with pitchforks dragged the vagrant into what looked like a giant millet mill to be crushed by its two slabs of stone while merrily singing a peasant song as they turned the mill round and round to grind him alive.

'Last but not least, the eighteenth level of hell, not that you would enjoy it, I assure you,' Hong Lian announced as she restored him with her last stalk of red lotuses in preparation for the torture, 'The Hell of Saws.'

At Hong Lian's behest, hordes of demonic effigies of all shapes and sizes grabbed their saws and rushed to the vagrant. The pain of dismemberment was compounded by multiple sawing all happening at once, not a scream could be heard—body or soul—from the poor man who had finally lost his mind in hell after his ordeal with the eighteen levels of extreme torture.

Those who found the vagrant's corpse sitting straight on a bench by the lake the next morning could only describe the bliss on his face, unaware that he had finally expunged all his karmic sins with the infamous eighteen hellish retributions that took place in his disturbed mind and troubled soul.

An owl's hooting brings relief,
to my yearning for lost love.
There I see my lover in grief,
knowing I had killed our love.

I came in with tears in the middle of the night to visit
Adrian Holmes at the Taiping Prison, not because I wanted
to, but because I had to. I was going crazy because of him,
my love for him was hurting me inside. Yes, I was missing
him more than life itself, and yet deep inside I didn't dare
to admit this after all the things I had done to him.

Like every woman in love, I had wanted my lover to
myself only—not willing to share him with his wife, and
certainly not with my twin, Hong Lian. He made every
love song I heard about us, and now even the heartbreak
ones were ours too. Could this love be just about us? Just
him and me?

There's nothing
more blissful
than falling in love.
There's nothing
more painful
than falling in love—
With whom
your heart belongs.

'You are here Pai Lian, I knew you would come,' Adrian Holmes said to me as he turned around from his bed and sat upright gently; unafraid of my presence, looking surprisingly elated that I was here. He looked tenderly at my face and asked the burning question that I had dreaded to hear, 'Why, my love?'

Tears fell down my cheeks and I cried my heart out. I came here bearing so much pain and I could not take it anymore. I came here because he was sad, and for that my heart started to break. My tears were words my heart couldn't express.

'Have I not loved you enough, Pai Lian?' Adrian asked me as tears welled up in his eyes before they came in endless streams, knowing mindless acts had destroyed his life. 'Do you not care for our love at all, my white lotus?'

'I am so sorry, Adrian, my love,' I sobbed profusely, feeling tired—tired of the constant judgement, tired of hiding our love, tired of staying strong, tired of dreaming of a life I would never have with him. 'I was angry with you for having an affair with my twin sister and getting her pregnant.'

There! I confessed it, I was jealous! What did Hong Lian have that I didn't? She was my twin after all! Granted that she didn't know about my affair with Adrian, but still, to bear his baby when I couldn't just broke my heart.

'Now, the world thinks I murdered your sister,' he said, trying to shut his eyes to stop the flow of tears—what he really hoped was to shut himself from the world—and then continued, 'A murder done by the book . . . my book, ghostwritten by you, imagine that.'

Guilt flared up and wreaked my heart, leaving me feeling empty and emotionally drained. I was drowning in regrets, haunted by pain and sorrow yet again. 'What have I done?' I screamed at myself. What was done, could never be undone!

Jealousy, it was. All I wanted was him—Adrian Holmes. Jealousy was the ugliest . . . jealousy was me; starting from my heart and ending with my sister's death. Now my beloved would be dead next. What should I do?

But like all good crime stories, there was always a twist.

'Did you really know the vagrant, Adrian?' I asked my lover point-blank, sighing with much sadness as I waited for his answer. In the book, the protagonist did.

Adrian Holmes froze.

'Baby, I wanted to save our love,' he said, crying hysterically and confessing his part in all this, 'Your sister was pregnant, and Marguerite Daisy would divorce me and take every cent I owned. It was in our pre-nuptial agreement!'

So the nameless vagrant had a name. Who was he? Did he have to die before we knew his name?

I did not know who was more guilty—I, for sending my twin sister to her death with a pearl necklace as a lure, or Adrian, who sent a crazy homeless vagrant to do his dirty job? Whose borrowed knife was deadlier?

'He was Anthony Homes, my half-brother from another mother,' Adrian revealed between sobs and confessed, 'He was abandoned at an orphanage by his ailing Malaysian mother when he was a child because he had a neurological disorder that was too costly to treat. I took advantage of Anthony's weaknesses to solve my dilemma.'

Why is he so comfortably admitting the truth to me?
I wondered. *Is it because I am complicit in the murder of my
twin sister as well? Or is it because I am a ghost and there
is nothing I can do about it?*

'You sent your twin sister to her death with the pearl
necklace as a lure,' Adrian reminded me of my guilt as
he reiterated his, 'I killed your twin by sending my crazy
brother after her.'

Both of us were guilty as hell—both of us taking a
page or two from our own crime novel! What remained
to be seen now was who would be the one to cast the
first stone.

'And then you tried to put the blame on me by passing
the inspector our book,' he continued, accusing me while
shaking his head in pure dismay and disbelief, 'while
I did nothing of that sort to you when I could . . . because
I love you.'

> Guilt falls unto me, silencing my heart,
> Smothering me in a heavy quilt of tears,
> I try exhaling my sins but I fall apart,
> Nothing will ease this pain I now fear.
>
> The rain won't wash away my tears,
> The night won't brighten my inner darkness.
> Too many wrongs to right, I now fear,
> Everything is slipping back into darkness.

'If you have ever loved me, save me from the hangman's
noose, please,' Adrian pleaded with me, knowing he had
me at *I love you*. He knew a million stars lit up my eyes
when I heard what my heart yearned to know, but he also

knew there were a million reasons for me to say *no* after the betrayal on his part. 'Please?' he repeated. 'Look, I didn't blame the murder on you like you did,' he gently reminded me, his voice hoarse and desperate this time, still trying to convince me of his love to sway me.

That has to count for something, I entertained the thought for a while, *he didn't do me any harm even after I inflicted so much damage unto him.*

'I admit I am still deeply in love with you,' I told Adrian with a sigh even though he knew that already. Although I very much wanted to destroy him for what he did to me, love was stronger than vengeance and I couldn't do it up to a point—only getting him arrested, which I regretted so much that I took my own life at the bridge in Taiping Botanical Garden. 'I just wanted you to know that I will make things right by getting you out of here because I still love you.'

'How, my white lotus?' Adrian asked me, his tear-stained face now beaming with hope. He had given up faith, it seemed, but with my help he could be saved, even though he didn't deserve my mercy one bit.

'I will make the confession and take all the blame, don't you worry,' I said, feeling uneasy on the inside knowing what I had to do. 'Just don't ask me how, please.'

Let the world hate me for all I care, it wasn't like I was innocent either. *Since I am already dead it wouldn't matter*, I reasoned with myself, *at least I can do something good for those who matter to me.*

15

18 December 1979

'So, what changed? Why the sudden change of heart?' Inspector Abdul Rahman asked Ernest Maxwell Graves after perusing the photocopies of Chang Pai Lian's latest chapters while taking a leisurely sip of his hot *ocha* in Sushi Momantai, a Japanese restaurant tucked away in Lorong Tupai, Taiping. An incredible eatery for seasonal fine dining, the restaurant was renowned for combining hospitality with artisanal skills that provided diners with a unique dining experience. Sometimes, a little overfriendly, the rotund man complained when he saw Ernest got all the attention from the wait-staff by virtue of him being so good-looking.

'May we offer you our oysters with *Tosazu* dressing?' the waitress asked, dressed up to the nines like a geisha hostess, straight from the Steven Spielberg's 2005 movie, *Memoirs of a Geisha*. She was clearly undressing Ernest with her eyes, the Inspector noticed, not that the clueless writer would know anyway. 'By the way, kind sir, I am Akina Ichiba-san and I am at your service,' she said with a wink.

'Nice to meet you, Ichibawa-san,' Ernest said to the waitress, mispronouncing her name and causing Inspector Abdul Rahman to cough up his hot *ocha* everywhere. A panic ensued as all the waitresses rushed to his side to clean up the mess.

'Not Ichibawa, it's Ichiba-san,' the Inspector corrected, aghast at the writer's knack of saying all the wrong things at the wrong time. With a huff, he turned to the waitress and said, 'Don't mind him, you can call him Takmaukasi-san.' A disappointed sigh was heard from all the waitresses, and they went about doing their chores with their hearts broken.

Unsure of what had just happened, Ernest decided to change the subject lest he would become a joke for being so clueless. It was better for him to steer the conversation back to the purpose of their meeting, he decided.

'Yeah, I know what you mean,' Ernest replied to the Inspector's earlier question as he took a bite of his hokkigai artic surf clam dipped in wasabi sauce. Pai Lian had wanted to exonerate Adrian Holmes from all the blame, and yet, here she was divulging everything they had done in a book that she was ghostwriting for Ernest. *What gives?* Ernest wondered.

'Maybe the question isn't *what changed* but *what happened?*' Ernest postulated, 'And I think Hong Lian happened, but Pai Lian has yet to write about it.'

'From what we know, everything Pai Lian wrote in the manuscript checks out,' the Inspector informed Ernest while stirring the *tentsuyu* sauce with grated *daikon* and ginger bits for his *tempura moriawase* spread, 'Yeah, even this prison visit episode.'

'I thought the visual and audio quality was abysmal?' a surprised Ernest asked the Inspector when he recalled their conversation at the Inspector's office the other day. If it was that bad, like what they saw, there was no point in submitting it as evidence. They could bet their last dollar that Adrian's legal team would fight to dismiss it. 'Can it be submitted in court?' he asked.

'The digital team in forensics has restored the evidence. Just so you know, we could hear the conversation clearly,' Inspector Abdul Rahman declared, happy that they got what they needed. He had this in his bag, he was sure, along with the promotion that he wanted. *How marvellous the technology is these days*, he thought gleefully, *Wrong doers, beware!*

Apparently, the team had been able to upscale the resolution of the video and adjust the frame rate, codec, aspect ratio, and bitrate. As for the audio, they were able to boost clarity with the available audio software.

With a big smile, he turned to Ernest and declared, 'With Adrian's own confession on file, he is toast!'

'That's great!' Ernest exclaimed jubilantly, although he couldn't help feeling a little scared. Things were going far too smoothly for him and if he knew the universe well, it rarely gave anyone free passes. There could be bumps ahead . . . big ones. 'You reckon we'll have trouble from Adrian's legal team?' Ernest asked the Inspector, a little worried things might go awry.

'Of course, that goes without saying,' Inspector Abdul Rahman replied aloud, but then casually added, 'Unexpectedly, we'll have to contend with trouble of another kind—the supernatural ones.'

'You think Pai Lian would come for this?' Ernest jested at the ridiculous notion, laughing loudly at the Inspector's expense. Then, a thought flashed past his mind, 'She did say she would spring her lover free, right? This could mean she would do anything to destroy this damning evidence, right? We are in danger, aren't we?' he asked nervously.

'Yes, but Marguerite Daisy wouldn't be happy if Pai Lian came for the evidence,' Inspector Abdul Rahman said with a smirk, and took a sip of his *hot ocha* before continuing, 'Remember, that woman stands to inherit her husband's great fortune when he dies and will possibly do anything and everything to protect it, even standing in Pai Lian's way if she has to.'

Ernest nodded in agreement as he savoured his delectable *tobiko* flying fish roe sushi and ruminated on the possibility. From what he could see, it was very likely that both the wife and the late mistress would come to blows—the former couldn't wait for her husband to die while the latter wanted her lover to live on out of guilt. And there standing in the line of fire was the evidence and a $100 million fortune at stake.

'Looks like we're going to die if we aren't careful about this,' Ernest groaned and shook his head.

'Could we interest you two to dice with death and try our *fugu* dishes?' Akina, the waitress, asked with a smile at the most inopportune moment. Both Inspector Abdul Rahman and Ernest Maxwell Graves looked at each other horrified, both thinking it was an inauspicious stroke of serendipity sent by the universe . . . death by a poisonous fish or death by ghost?

'No, thank you,' they declined, simultaneously reaching for the salt to throw over their shoulders, not quite ready to tempt death any time soon.

16

At the Rain Café in Jalan Maharajalela, a tired Ernest Maxwell Graves sank his body into a plush velvety sofa, easing the sweltering heat of the day away with the cooling breeze of the establishment's air conditioner. The rejuvenating cold rush of his favourite ice-blended macchiato quenched his parched throat while his ears were seduced by the swing-style rhythmic syncopations and accents of Billie Holiday's glorious songs from yesteryears.

In a quiet corner of the café, a gentle table lamp glowed lazily like a glorious sunset next to a painting by Frida Kahlo, probably bought from a private collector residing in Cayoacán, Mexico, which strangely brought to mind his carefree summers in Ibiza during happier times. With an indolent sigh, he took a sip of his coffee before reading the new pages of the manuscript left by the White Lotus ghost.

> Oh, will it ever get better,
> This cruel pain inside of me?
> Oh, does it ever get better,
> This loneliness killing me?
>
> God knows I have to let go,
> The Devil won't let you go.

> Memories flood my mind,
> Love putting me in a bind.

A lovelorn ghost, torn in life and in death, Ernest thought of Chang Pai Lian, *a sadness beyond all telling, her happiness could only be found in love.* He pitied her for finding love that could not see the light of day—he was a married man; he pitied her for holding out for a love that would die with the waning moon because her man would never leave his wife. *A lovelorn ghost whose mind won't erase the memories that they had made.*

If truth be told, he pitied her for having a heart that was slow to learn what her mind had quickly come to know—that this love of hers could never be. She would be better off with any other man surely, if she ever wanted a chance at love, he would imagine.

> If I rip my heart out in exasperation,
> Will your love come my way?
> If my sad tears rain in desperation,
> Will your love save the day?

Chang Pai Lian's devotion to Adrian Holmes was admirable in a wrong way, bordering on infatuation; no, make that obsession. Was this why she had visited him in prison, after being hell-bent on crushing him for impregnating and murdering her twin sister?

> I had a fight with my sister,
> She didn't know what it was about,
> One word led to another,
> His love made us fall out.

Surprise, surprise, surprise . . . in this chapter, Chang Pai Lian indicated she knew about her twin sister's affair with her lover, Adrian, *before* the murder, which made her suspect No. 1. But was that what she wanted them to think so she could exonerate her lover from blame and free him? At this very juncture, no one could really tell because the plots had now swayed off-tangent. *A Bridge to Murderville* was a mystery crime thriller, but his book was starting to inadvertently become a horror fantasy.

Wasn't this what Inspector Abdul Rahman had wanted to know? Should he be told about this? Would this unravel the case he was working on? But would the words of a ghost stand in court? Didn't the police have DNA of the baby in Hong Lian's womb? More conclusive, no? The motive for the murder clear and irrefutable, yes?

Headache plagued Ernest's mind, how would this case turn out?

Well, first things first, he had to talk to the inspector about this to ascertain the next steps. Was that what Pai Lian had wanted him to do? It was not like she didn't know he was seeing the inspector to help her bring Adrian Holmes to justice. What now? In an about turn, it looked like Adrian Holmes was about to get away scot-free.

Sick with worry, Ernest beckoned the waiter for his bill before leaving the Rain Café to see Inspector Abdul Rahman. As he opened the door, he realized it had started raining. A thought flashed past his mind—heaven was weeping for the poor White Lotus ghost with her unending tribulations. *No, thank you, he would wait for a little while. No reason to catch a cold and get sick when things needed getting done,* he reasoned.

17

Marguerite Daisy Holmes wanted it discreet, and discreet was what she got—hiding from the paparazzi, having tea with Lady Nightshade in a secretive corner at Heavenly Eden Tea House located at Persiaran, Taiping. She had specifically chosen this establishment in view that it was patronized by the elite of society and was out of bounds for the less privileged and economically challenged.

Who could afford Da-Hong Pao, a type of oolong tea, valued at a whopping $1.2 million per kilogram? It was reputedly grown in the Wuyi mountains of Fujian province in China and declared a national treasure for its rarity—the best one came from the great mother trees of which only six existed on the planet. Just twenty grams of Da-Hong Pao tea would cost around $30,000, a sum that the likes of Marguerite Daisy could very well afford.

This evening, there were only a few esteemed guests, Marguerite Daisy noticed—on her far left, she spotted the handsome billionaire, Gerald, a shipping tycoon with a dark penchant for sadomasochism; and on her far right, there was Kok Yu, the billionaire genius who created an accounting software that the world was using. The latter was looking apprehensively at them while whispering something into the ears of his tycoon friend Wea Fung who owned hotel resorts in Chiang Mai, Bangkok, and Shanghai.

She would have loved to say hello to them in person, but she knew it was an unwise thing to do since Lady Nightshade had a falling out with them in Heavenly Eden eons ago . . . so much worse than the infamous Boston Tea Party, she laughed at Lady Nightshade's expense.

These billionaires weren't angels either, barring Lady Nightshade from Heavenly Eden like that. It was only by the virtue of her sheer presence that they tolerated Lady Nightshade in the tea house for now. Obviously, they knew who she was and loathed to create a scene. *Best to ignore them*, Marguerite Daisy decided, *lest feelings be hurt*.

'How is your tea?' Lady Nightshade asked Marguerite Daisy, eyeing the liquid gold encased in a shell-shaped dark-green jade cup, mounted in pure gold and enamelled exquisitely. As generous as Marguerite Daisy was, the psychic medium was only treated to Panda Dung tea, reportedly first cultivated by An Yanshi in southwest China. It was sold at approximately $70,000 per kilogram, still not a sum to be sniffed at. 'You know I am well versed in tasseography, the art of reading tea leaves, right?'

'Yes, dear,' Marguerite Daisy replied, wondering why her psychic medium liked stating the obvious. Afterall, wasn't it why they were here in the first place? Wasn't she asked to consume the tea and swirl the loose leaves while contemplating her question? Like all divination practices, it was based on the concept of redirecting thought energies. The tea leaves were supposed to be energetic conduits that were capable of mirroring past, present, and future. 'Done drinking it,' Marguerite Daisy said and passed the precious jade cup to her psychic medium, eagerly awaiting the verdict. 'What does it say?'

'Let me see,' Lady Nightshade said, taking the jade cup by the handle with her left hand, rim upwards, and moved it in a circle rapidly three times from left to right—some of the loose tea leaves clung to the sides of the jade cup while others remained at the bottom. In a deft move, she inverted the cup over its jade saucer, leaving the last bits of the liquid to drain away so she could interpret the signs. 'Let's get our bearings first so we can start,' she said.

The handle of the jade cup represented Marguerite Daisy in her own sphere and was the south point of the compass. The cup was divided into three parts—the rim designated the present; the sides, events in the near future; and the bottom, events in the distant future. The challenge was to identify the symbols left by the tea leaves in these parts to decipher the divination.

'I see a broken heart near the handle,' Lady Nightshade said as she turned the cup to view the symbol from every angle, squinting her eyes for a good look every now and then. 'And that's you, Marguerite dear. It is not something we aren't aware of, is it?'

Broken hearts, broken marriages, those were her lot in life, Marguerite Daisy rued her fate, no thanks to all those affairs that her previous husbands had, including the current one that had devastated her so terribly. Inevitably she was left with scars upon her broken heart with only great fortunes to assuage her pain.

'I didn't pay you to tell me something I already know,' she answered testily, her feelings hurt having to come to terms with the uncomfortable truth. 'What does the rest say?' she asked the psychic medium impatiently, hoping for better news.

'Sorry, love, bad news,' Lady Nightshade replied, a tad too happy that Marguerite Daisy got the short end of fate. *This would hopefully teach Miss High and Mighty to be less rude*, she thought gleefully while laughing to herself.

'I see a caged bird upside down. Somebody confessed something and will die because of it,' the psychic medium said, 'Your husband, Adrian Holmes, must have confessed his sins while in prison. He will die because of it.'

'How is that bad news?' Marguerite Daisy retorted haughtily and laughed aloud. *Let him die for his stupidity*, she thought, *like I could care less?* 'He dies and I inherit his fortune,' she said to a surprised Lady Nightshade. *Well, the man invariably deserves his death after what he has done to me, and I unequivocally deserve his fortune for all the hurt he has caused me,* she reasoned with herself.

Lady Nightshade was taken aback for a moment, not expecting Marguerite Daisy to be this cold. Gone was the image of the latter being a victim in her mind. *Damn, is this coming from someone who played victim in reel life and in real life? Well, no longer!*

'As for the event in the far future, I see a skull at the bottom of your cup,' Lady Nightshade told Lady Marguerite. This inevitably involved a spectre of some sort. Trying to destroy the evidence perhaps? To set the bird free from its cage maybe? 'Hmm . . . the tea leaves are telling me that a ghost will try to rectify the situation,' the psychic medium disclosed her concerns to Marguerite Daisy, 'I think she is attempting to spring your husband free from prison.'

'Now, that is bad news,' Marguerite Daisy exclaimed, anxiety working up her blood pressure. If this bastard of a husband were set free somehow, she would have to kiss his fortune goodbye forever. What could she do to prevent this? What would Mummy do?

'I have to prevent this ghost from destroying the evidence, even if that's the last thing I do,' she swore vehemently. A bane of her life—first as her husband's mistress, and now as a 'ghostly' hinderance. *Oh, when will I be able to get rid of my competition once and for all?* she wondered.

'I'll call for the bill for our tea,' Marguerite Daisy hurried the psychic medium as she hastily grabbed her Mouawad 1001 Nights diamond purse, currently retailing at $3.8 million in the market. *There is much to be done, Mummy would know what to do.* Murdering people and ghosts wasn't Marguerite's cup of tea but it was certainly her mother's!

'By the way what has become of Hong Lian?' Marguerite Daisy asked Lady Nightshade, wondering aloud what the Red Lotus ghost was up to since they put her on the path to their enemies, 'Did she have any luck in destroying my nemeses, besides the vagrant?'

'Ah yes, you already know what happened to the homeless vagrant,' the psychic medium said, secure in the knowledge that the crazy man had been dealt with and had perished in all ways that counted. Oh, how he must have suffered! 'But you'd want to know this, something had happened to Hong Lian when she met Pai Lian.'

PART II

Of Sister Dearest and Mending Bridges

Night becometh my sister, a nightmare she now is,
Murdered by a borrowed knife, drowned in a lake,
Deadly is my jealousy, deadlier still her lover's kiss,
Too much to be forgiven, apologies now are too late.

For a drowned sister's sake, I'd die a thousand times,
My body stained with tears, my soul soaked in sins.
Night knows my regrets, now I'm crying for all times,
Come end me by the lake, before hell takes my sins.

Under the blood moon by the lake in Taiping Botanical Garden, I waited for my sister to come see me and exact her revenge. Since I woke up from my death, I had felt the ominous dark remorse—brought on by my terrible guilt—prick my conscience.

Memories took me to the days in our mother's womb, when I first saw my reflection in my twin, joining me in prefect likeness right down to our spirits; both of us together in darkness with no fear of being alone. She reached out to me, hugging me, and in her touch, I felt the bond of twins and her promise that we would be there for each other until the end of time.

Like lotuses from the same pond, like birds of the same feather, my twin and I were always together when we were young—sharing the laughter and the tears, united together with no fear—until in adulthood, a man and a pregnancy came between us.

I killed our eternal sisterly bond, bound by blood that I had spilt so callously in a fit of cruel jealousy. As twins, we weren't expected to ask for permission to become each other's best memories, and as sisters, we were expected to share our hearts and live our best lives together. I had failed her miserably, having broken her heart and in a way, taken her life.

'You are here at long last, like you promised you would,' I remarked, tears flowing down my cheeks when I finally sensed Hong Lian's presence watching me from beyond the raintrees—a feat made possible by the bond that twins shared, ours reignited once again when we came in close proximity of each other, thank the heavens!

Here, the two of us again, still together in darkness, still without the fear of being alone—only this time in death, not in life . . .

Forgive me if I cry again, for I knew nothing else I could do with so many terrible things that had happened between us. I know, I know . . . crying wouldn't change anything nor wash away everything that I had done.

Oh, if only my tears could fill back the hole in my soul. Oh, if only fate had warned me of what my life would be without her.

But deep in me, I already knew my fate and my sins would sooner or later summon me hither, to where I would face my sister's judgment.

Right on cue, I heard my twin sister, Hong Lian, sing from beyond the raintrees, struggling with the aches in her head from hitting the stone in the lotus pond; her song a hollow echo from the wound in her heart caused by the dagger from a borrowed knife.

Why can't I think straight?
My thoughts can't find words.
Why can't I feel right?
Her dagger feels like a sword.

Oh, my dear Hong Lian, my Red Lotus! How I've missed her beautiful voice and her lovely songs. I could never forget her talent for the Beijing opera in a hundred lifetimes—a gift from the heavens when she was alive, reaffirmed with gifts of operatic paper effigies from me when she was dead. To hear her sing again brought much joy to my heart, even though I knew great pain would soon follow, judging from the operatic despair in her songs.

Lured with lies and a promise of love,
Alone, I waited by the moonlit lotus lake.
Lured by pearls, a killer made his move;
Alone, I died with my loveless soul to take.

Dusk crying to the dawn, my sister betrayed me;
Sending me to my death with pearls on my neck.
Stars screaming at the moon, my lover killed me;
Sending a crazy man, now my body was a wreck.

All their vicious deeds like hell so low,
My vengeance was fire to help them burn.
For all my bitter tears they had let flow,
Now to suffer and die I swore their turn.

With a dramatic display of her acrobatic skills honed from years of practice on stage, Hong Lian somersaulted deftly in all her operatic splendour—clad in a lady warrior's red regalia—landing on a raintree branch while paper effigies made their entrance playing *jinghu* and *erhu* fiddles, *yuequin* mandolin, as well as *pipa* and *xianzi* lutes.

> Hell comes knocking with vengeance,
> You'll pay for all the hurt and the pain.
> Cry in the dirt and suffer in your penance,
> Die now with the evils that hell will rain.

With exaggerated twirling from branch to branch, she swirled her sleeves to reveal hidden twin blades as *suona* horns, *jingbo* cymbals, *paiban* clappers, and *tanggu* drums filled the night air, scaring the roosting birds to death and bringing tears to the weeping willows by the lake.

'My sister, Pai Lian, how could you have the heart to kill me?!' Hong Lian yelled bitterly with hot tears streaking down her made-up cheeks—a ghastly sight to behold—while throwing her heartbreaking accusation like a dart at me and drawing first blood, 'Knowing fully well I was with child!'

If there ever was a time to love, it was now or never. Innocence was no longer a contention after what I had done, sending my twin sister to her death with pearls on her neck like she said I had. If there ever was a time to fight, it was now or never. She might have stolen my lover and gotten pregnant unknowingly, but all fight had left me, and I no longer had the strength to explain my side of the story . . . as though that would exonerate me after what I had done to her!

'If my death could bring you solace, so be it,' I told Hong Lian sadly, preferring her to end me there and then. My guilt had built me a prison in my mind and my soul, and I would be free with a slash or two from her blades.

Why would I want her to suffer the guilt of knowing I was her lover's lover first and her child was a mockery of my love for Adrian Holmes? Like I hadn't done her enough harm. What was the point of letting her suffer the guilt when I already wanted to end mine once and for all? Don't worry, my dear beloved sister, I would carry both of our guilts to my grave, so you didn't have to.

She said blood was thicker than water. I could be the living example of that with my death. She could kill me and my blood would be a proof of that. 'Kill me, if it means ending your suffering once and for all,' I said with much love and closed my eyes to stem my tears in acceptance of my fate.

Right on cue, the operatic crescendo built up with the ear-piercing wail of *suona* double-reed instrument and the clashing of *jingbo* cymbals in tandem with the deafening echoes of *daluo* bending gongs. Hong Lian somersaulted onto the ground and did acrobatic flips with her twin blades towards me while the *tanggu* drums droned on mercilessly.

With both blades crisscrossed and locked onto my jugulars, Hong Lian suddenly stopped short of killing me at the last minute and began to waver with doubts at my unflinching resolve in the face of death.

Her red lips quivered nervously, and she asked me bluntly after a pregnant pause, 'Why won't you fight?' Subconsciously, a fog was lifted from her mind with the passing of her headaches, and she saw the truth in my tears, which reignited the bond that twins like us shared and cherished.

'W . . . Why? Why didn't you tell me?' Hong Lian sobbed in frustration, ashamed that she had done me irreparable harm first by unknowingly having an illicit

affair with my lover and then getting pregnant as a
result. The sudden realization of this painful knowledge
had regrettably left her with an uneasy sinking feeling,
much like drowning in quicksand, I sensed.

Deep inside me, I knew she felt guilty for ripping apart
my heart, guilty without measure for ruining my life . . .
and hers as well. 'I . . . I am so sorry, my dear sister,
my White Lotus,' she cried torrents, sorry that we sisters
were both in this sad predicament together.

Dropping both blades onto the ground with a loud
clang, she suddenly hugged me like the time we were in
our mother's womb as both of us burst into tears anew;
our pain dissipating between our arms, her selfless act
reconciling our hurt, flaws, and all—bringing to light our
dark secrets along with the uncomfortable truths that we
had covered with lies.

'Had I known he was yours in the first place, I wouldn't
have pursued his love even if it pained me so,' a teary
Hong Lian confessed to me, regretting the affair that
ushered the beginning of our end. 'Had I known, even if
there was a remote chance of my knowing, I would still
give you my blessings for your union. Know this, dear
sister, that I'd rather be buried in your arms than be
loved by him,' she told me, sobbing.

'Hush, the fault is all mine, and this sin is mine to
bear alone,' I told Hong Lian, grief-stricken to see the
pain in my sister's eyes as a part of my heart died with
her sadness. No matter how hard I tried, all I did was
made her cry.

What I did was unforgivable, I knew that in my heart.
In my jealousy, I had sent my beloved sister, Hong Lian,
to her death—I failed to cherish her, failed to protect her,

failed to put her first. Only when I had bared my soul in an act of self-sacrifice did my sister bare her heart selflessly, paving the way for a surprise reconciliation.

'I'm so sorry, please forgive me, dear sister,' I wept profusely, knowing my guilt wouldn't tolerate any excuses and my remorse couldn't hide no more. Secrets lie, secrets kill. Like it or not, I had to assume full accountability for all that I had done and atone for all my misdeeds. 'There's no point in crying over spilled milk . . . or blood in our case.'

But there was still one big issue that I needed to deal with—Adrian Holmes—now that our secrets were out in the open. 'How do you want me to deal with your lover who had you and your baby killed?' I asked Hong Lian aloud, mentally tired and emotionally drained, sickened to my core with the consequences that secrets wrought.

Close your ears, you whispering trees!
The ears of roosting birds steal secrets.
They hear what we say, flying away free!
They sing anyway, causing us regrets.

'My love for him died with me and my baby,' Hong Lian wept and told me, dismayed that a love like hers would be sacrificed for her lover's financial interests. He had wanted to protect his fortune lest his divorce would take everything he had to his wife, Marguerite Daisy, on grounds of infidelity. Love didn't win the day, it lost. And consequently, she and her baby lost their lives at the cost of this love, too high a price to pay. 'W . . . We've already sinned too much, and there have been many deaths,' she mourned sadly, her pain visibly apparent on her expression, 'Let's show him the mercy he didn't accord us.'

Ahh . . . perhaps love did win the day, or night in this case, just not the way everyone expected. In the plight of loving Adrian Holmes, we sisters bled and willingly surrendered ourselves to death, for with it came merciful emancipation. He didn't know love, this Adrian Holmes, but we did. There was no reasoning with love, however flawed the object of our desire sadly was. In all truth, I didn't think we had it in us to kill him, even though he very well deserved it in all ways that counted. I certainly couldn't.

'He is currently incarcerated in Taiping Prison and will be on death row if he loses his trial,' I updated Hong Lian on the gravity of Adrian Holmes' dangerous situation. 'There was his confession to me that the authorities had on file, which will be his undoing. If we were to intervene, that evidence must be destroyed.'

'Be warned, sister, for danger stands in our way,' Hong Lian said to me as she shared her side of the saga. 'His wife will do everything she can to prevent this from happening since she stands to lose his fortune if he survives this case. And she has an advantage with the ghost of her mother, Madam Petunia Yates, and the psychic medium, Lady Nightshade, on her side.'

It was sheer dumb luck that she had bested Madam Petunia Yates and the psychic medium the other time, Hong Lian told me—her sheer madness at that time surprised them, or was it that they had let her win so they could send her on a rampage to do their work? One would never really know, but it stood to reason they were capable of doing such things. They played the long game, and we could be short-sighted for not seeing their plans well in advance.

After all, didn't they let me have the accursed South Sea pearl necklace on purpose? Marguerite Daisy had hoped for the ghost of her mother to eliminate me, even though she didn't really know I was the mistress at that time. They didn't count on the fact that I gave the pearl necklace away to my twin, Hong Lian. But the accursed pearl necklace did work, luring the crazy vagrant to murder my sister with its curse. I didn't count on the fact that Adrian Holmes had also sent his half-brother to end Hong Lian at that time, which—surprise, surprise, surprise—was the unwitting crazy vagrant all along!

A web of intrigue passion weaves,
Ensnaring us like none other.
Sinking poison, send your wreath,
Death comes, we die together.

Like a spider weaving its web between stalks of flowers, sooner or later we would all get ensnared, I lamented. Why did I get the feeling that Adrian was the unwitting spider weaving his web of passion and lies, entangling us sisters, White Lotus and Red Lotus, along with the likes of Marguerite Daisy, Madam Petunia Yates, and Lady Nightshade.

Oh dear, dear me! Will the spider ever get ensnared in its own web? I wondered. *What if it didn't, then we all die, yes? What then, we send wreaths of flowers to ourselves?*

'Earth to Pai Lian!' Hong Lian shrieked in utter terror, waking me from my daydreaming to a nightmare of diabolical proportions, 'In case you didn't notice, hell has come for us!'

Echoing her panic, the *Diyu* realm of the dead opened before us with blizzards raging and thunder roaring—a purgatory to punish and purify souls for reincarnation by cleansing sins with varying degrees of torture in hell first before drinking Granny Meng Po's Broth of oblivion and crossing the Naihe Bridge of Forgetfulness to be reborn.

'No, no, no . . .' I protested in fear, knowing both of us had sins to pay for when our time on earth was up. Wait! There was a forty-nine-day leeway right after death before judgment commenced. I hadn't exhausted mine yet, having been dead for just over a fortnight, but it wasn't the case for my beloved twin, Hong Lian. Today, it was exactly forty-nine days after her murder on 1st November!

Oh my sister! We just got reunited and now we would part again, I wailed inside. *Where in hell would I ever meet her again? I don't want to lose her again . . . I won't, not after all the wrongs I have done to her!*

Where in hell was the question indeed! If I recalled Chinese folk religion correctly, there were 12,800 hells located under this earth of ours—eight dark hells, eight cold hells, and 84,000 miscellaneous hells located at the edge of the universe. *Oh, sister dear, were we doomed to be forever apart?*

Before I lost my wits to despair, there was something even more frightening—every soon-to-be-dead soul walking into hell was escorted by two guardians, in her case it was Ox Head and Horse Face, two infamous wardens of hell, alongside ghoulish officials of dark justice equipped with terrible weapons of torture.

Resistance was futile as all eyes from Heaven and Hell were upon us. If we fought, it was akin to resisting arrest, not that we poor souls could ever hope to win, even if we worked together. We would only bring undue problems unto ourselves—our one and only chance for reincarnation forfeited and be forever condemned to the eighteenth level of *Diyu*, the deepest hell from where there's no escape. That would be akin to *Naraka*, or the *Avici* and *Jahanam* hell if anyone cared to know or compare.

'Stand forth and kneel, Chang Hong Lian, the condemned soul designated for *Diyu* by the edict of The Ten Yama Kings,' bellowed Ox Head, who was clad in his traditional armour and, as expected, had the head of an ox with huge, sharp horns. 'Your heinous sins merit hell; it was a mistake eighteen times over for executing a vagrant so unlawfully.'

'I concur and agree, you will be bound and whipped along the way to hell,' Horse Face said in a neighing nasal tone, the counterpart warden to Ox Head, having checked the registry of condemned souls for verification. As his name suggested, he had the head of a horse and was armed to the teeth with hellish weapons. 'Surrender quietly and offer no resistance because you wouldn't want to cross path with the *Heibai Wuchang* guardians.'

The names of these duo struck fear in our hearts—they were the Black and White Guardians of hell, literally 'Black and White Impermanence' deities who could wipe souls out with a thought. Fear was seeing their black and white shadows coming to claim souls on deathbed for hell, it was said. Reassuringly, they only came for souls of deities and demons, not humans unless bigger threats were expected.

'Diyu?!' I wailed in horror and wondered what my twin sister had done in her moment of madness, not that I was any better. It was I who had sent Hong Lian to her death with pearls on her neck, later murdered by a vagrant sent by Adrian Holmes. A knock on her head from hitting a stone at the bottom of the lake caused her insanity. Surely she wasn't to blame, was she?

But she really did take the law into her hands and took a life that was not hers to take.

Now, whatever she inflicted onto the poor man would be hers to suffer alone, eighteen times over. 'No, she has suffered enough,' I cried. I needed to save my sister at all costs!

Hell is where her immortal soul goes,
Time for redemption has long passed.
Eternal torture she will have to undergo,
Stairway to heaven, she will not pass.

I did her wrong, my heart's broken,
Suffer I must, my atonement is here.
Her tortures will now be my burden,
Nightmares won't even take me there.

I sprang into action and stepped forth—kneeling before the wardens, Ox Head and Horse Face, impersonating my twin sister while praying no one would notice, 'I am Chang Hong Lian and I surrender my soul to be judged.'

A wave of horror swept Hong Lian's face but before she could say anything to jeopardize my plan, I gave her a stern warning with my eyes to shut her mouth. Before Ox Head and Horse Face could react, the legion of ghoulish hell officials clamoured unto me and hurriedly shackled me with burning handcuffs and chains. Hong Lian's eyes filled with tears when she saw how I suffered on her behalf.

'Argh . . .' I screamed in pain as they proceeded to drag me into the hellish portal where they came from, lashing me with bullwhips made of human rawhide and braided with multiple blades at their tips. *Crack, crack,*

crack, the bullwhips went furiously, causing me to scream in pain and Hong Lian to faint from panic. And then, with a ghastly fervour that could turn the owls and the bats mad, the ghoulish hell officials began to sing in eerie merriment.

Painfully, so painfully, we drag her to hell along,
She'll wilt like a flower in the wake of our song.
Rots like a dying petal on the ripples of a stream,
Cries like a banshee that forgets how to dream.

Agonizingly, so agonizingly, she'll burn in hell,
She'll suffer like a broken doll in a dark rotten cell.
Hangs like a string of pearls and falls like a tear,
Dies eighteen times over, sins too terrible to bear.

Then, something happened—the legion of ghoulish hell officials had trouble dragging me into the portal despite using all their strength and will power. The earth cracked and protested underneath me, pulling me away as the legion tried their best to push me in, but to no avail.

'You fools!' Ox Head bellowed loudly in anger at the legion, chastising his minions for their mistake. *Where in hell did they get these guys*, he couldn't help but wondered. 'You got the wrong twin. This one's time isn't up yet!'

'Don't think you can fool us with your martyrdom, Pai Lian,' Horse Face censured me in his neighing nasal tone, still holding on to his registry of condemned souls while reminding me of my dire situation, 'Your time will come soon enough after your forty-nine days.'

'Hell beckons, there is no god above to whom you can pray or turn to now,' Ox Head announced with a thunderous bellow, flogging my unfortunate twin, Hong Lian with his *Niu Wang* bullwhip and waking her up with a piercing scream—it magically fused with her soul, making it nigh impossible for her to escape with no way back or out, 'Cry for the sins of the dead for there is hell to pay!'

'Sister, help me!' Hong Lian screamed in breathless gasps of terror as she was dragged into the dark hellish portal that was now glowing red, where creeping shadows of utter dread relentlessly fought to rip her apart and gnash her with their claws and fangs. 'Somebody help me, please,' she wailed with tears of blood gushing down her cheeks.

'No . . .' I howled in protest, my pain apparent to all in heaven and hell. I scrambled desperately to grab her hands despite being handcuffed and chained by burning shackles, while crying my heart out, 'Leave her alone, take me, take me . . . for it was I who turned her to sin!'

'Nay, not now, for your suffering will come, rest assured,' Horse Face said and with a wave of his hand, my burning handcuffs and shackles disappeared along with my wounds, 'Make no mistake, Pai Lian. You are already marked for hell. Your window of redemption ends in a month.'

There was nothing I could do, I cried to all in heaven, earth, and hell as I watched my beloved twin sister disappear from this reality before my eyes. To lose someone whom I had wronged—the loss, the grief, the utter despair were all too much to bear. Bereavement was the feeling of nothingness in a whirlwind of pain, an endless bleakness akin to drought with a dry wind's bite!

My grief consumed me and I needed to live my truth. May the words I penned set me free from my pain and my guilt before my hell takes over.

18

23 December 1979

It was only when the rain stopped after Maghrib prayer time that Ernest Maxwell Graves and Inspector Abdul Rahman reached Bomoh Mona Mawar's residence in Kampung Lidin, Taiping, Perak. Hers was a traditional Malay mansion styled like a *rumah perabung lima*, complete with raised floor on stilts, and a large overhang roof piled with *singgora* tiles.

Both men had trudged through muddy puddles on the dirt road while being serenaded by a croaking chorus of frogs along the way, and brushing away the silken spider webs with pearly dews on the branches of rambutan trees on the way every now and then. By the time they reached their destination, they were panting from exertion as they stood under the eaves of the immense roof that was still trickling with loose raindrops.

'Why are we doing this again?' Ernest asked the Inspector, forgetting the reason for a moment why they had sought the help of a renowned witch doctor in the first place. Oh yeah, now he recalled—they needed supernatural protection against a possible threat from Pai Lian. (Not that Ernest needed any, or so he thought.)

The Inspector, being a superstitious man, had insisted as he was afraid of the day when Pai Lian would come for the evidence and put his life at risk. There were no guarantees that she wouldn't come looking for it, so he had to play it safe . . . with a little help from Bomoh Mona Mawar to stay safe at all costs.

'I read her latest chapter you sent me,' Inspector Abdul Rahman disclosed to Ernest, still traumatized by the terrifying events described in it. Didn't both sisters decide to save Adrian Holmes? How would that make it safe for him? Granted, one was thrown into hell already, but the other wasn't!

'Don't forget Pai Lian wrote it in the book that she would come for the evidence,' the Inspector reminded Ernest vehemently. Well, if Ernest won't do anything about it, he would. Could Ernest not see the writing was already on the wall? Well, in this case, in the book!

'How much more warning do you need?' he asked Ernest bluntly, a little exasperated with the latter. 'Very likely, Pai Lian won't back down from the decision, not when both the sisters decided to show mercy before one was thrown into hell.'

'Can't you just back up the evidence on Cloud or something?' Ernest asked the inspector with an incredulous grin, shaking his head at the man for not taking the obvious technology route. The Taiping police department had advanced tech support, for God's sake!

Ironically, he was the one suggesting this when he himself was still using a mechanical typewriter, not that anyone would understand. Mind you, his typewriter had sentimental value—it used to belong to his late mother who wrote all her bestsellers with it.

'What makes you think that I haven't done that already?' the inspector retorted back, rolling his eyes in frustration. This *ang mo* just didn't get it, they were dealing with supernatural threats that necessitated a similar paranormal counter response. How would tech hold up against a spell that could erase evidence? Or magic that could alter reality? 'Nope, nope, nope, not taking any chances,' he declared adamantly.

'Gentlemen, gentlemen . . . so sorry I took so long,' Bomoh Mona Mawar apologized to both men, halting their discussion with her grand entrance. She was dressed to the nines, her hair looking like it was coiffured by Vidal Sassoon's shampoo girl.

'I was making *nasi kangkang* but *dah jadi bubur pulak*!' she chuckled, winking at them and expecting both men to laugh at her joke about her tardiness but all she got was their shocked expressions at her fabulousness. *Oh, they didn't get the joke*, she thought; but the fact was, that they hadn't come across a witch doctor as outlandish and flamboyant as she was.

'Why are you standing outside in the rain? *Sila masuk*,' she beckoned them, ushering them up to the porch and into her ostentatious living room with gilded and gaudy furniture while surreptitiously eyeing Ernest. *Ooo . . . a looker this one*, she thought and wondered where she had kept her love potion. 'Take a seat and refreshments will be served shortly,' she told them while making her way into the kitchen.

'Y . . . You sure she is a witch doctor?' Ernest asked the inspector, very much surprised that Bomoh Mona Mawar wasn't what he had pictured in his mind. He had expected her to look like an old hag—one with a black cat and a blacker cauldron, but she was more like a celebrity with endorsement contracts for Gulati Textile Store and Sofy sanitary pads. 'S . . . She looks astonishingly well preserved for someone in her sixties,' he remarked.

'Well, rumours have it that Bomoh Mona Mawar practiced the forbidden art of *susuk*, a type of dark magic conceived to preserve youth and beauty,' the inspector replied to Ernest, pleased to share what little he knew about the forbidden practices in his community. 'I really wouldn't be surprised if there's a gold needle with a diamond embedded in her chin somewhere.'

'Here you go, *minum-minum* for you gentlemen,' Bomoh Mona Mawar said as she walked back into her living room, carrying an antique Malay silver tray with two mocktails—one served with a rose on the rim of the glass and the other, an orchid. Unbeknown to both men, the drink with the rose was spiked with a dose of love potion meant to ensnare Ernest in her amorous trap.

'*Ambil satu*,' she offered Ernest, strategically edging the glass with the rose closer to him, but as fate would have it, Inspector Abdul Rahman unwittingly took it instead when Ernest hesitated due to language barrier. *Celaka betul*, Bomoh Mona Mawar lamented deep inside her heart, shaking her head in disbelief of her fate, *Why the fat one? Why me?*

Tak apa, she told herself, making a mental note to slip a bottle of love potion into Ernest's pants before he left for the evening—a dream had told her to do so, not that she was one to argue with providence. Anyway, one way or another, she would have her way with Ernest, she swore. As for the fat one, she could easily give him a counter potion if he misbehaved, she decided before taking a seat by their side.

'Story me,' Bomoh Mona Mawar urged the men to fill her in on their predicament, not too bothered about her less-than-perfect command of the English language. After all, clients came to her not for English lessons, but for her to aid them with her witchcraft. '*Cakap I* everything so I *boleh bantu dengan* problem you, whatever it is,' she implored the men to tell her the whole story so she could help them with their issues, no matter what those might be.

'Are you good with ridding a ghost from interfering with a police case?' Inspector Abdul Rahman asked Bomoh Mona Mawar. Well yes, he knew her from reputation, everybody in Taiping did. She was said to be a formidable witch doctor with clients coming to her from far and wide, but reputation could sometimes be misleading. Understandably, not many people were what they advertised. The last thing he needed was a fraudster mucking up his case. It won't just put his coveted promotion at risk, but their lives as well.

'Am I good?' Bomoh Mona Mawar reiterated Inspector Abdul Rahman's question with an arched eyebrow, a little sensitive over being quizzed with a question like that. In answer to that, she waved her left hand over an empty vase and stalks of roses started sprouting up. To the Inspector's utter amazement, one of the roses turned into a butterfly and flew away. 'Does that answer your question?' she asked Inspector Abdul Rahman cryptically while grinning cheekily.

'Oh you're good,' Inspector Abdul Rahman declared, coughing a little from embarrassment while passing a dossier he had prepared to Bomoh Mona Mawar. He was crestfallen when he saw the witch doctor had problems reading the English text. How would he explain the case to her then? It would take all night if he were to verbally brief her!

As it very well turned out, he was worried needlessly. Unfazed by the stack of heavily worded documents, Bomoh Mona Mawar casually grabbed Inspector's drink from his hand and muttered a spell before spitting into it. With an intense concentration marked by furrowed brows, she poured the drink all over the documents—her mind soaking up the contents from the damp pages in an instant. It was as though she had expended much saliva reading the texts aloud!

'*I tahu apa korang nak,*' she said matter-of-factly knowing just what was needed, and walked into the kitchen briefly before reappearing with two coconuts in her hands, an act that was met with much dismay. It was not too long ago that other shamans had also used coconuts as part of their repertoire and were heavily ridiculed for it. And now, coconuts again, raising doubts on Bomoh Mona Mawar's much vaunted skills.

'What? *Apa you orang tengok I macam ni?*' she asked aloud, puzzled that Inspector Abdul Rahman and Ernest were looking at her like she was an idiot or something . . . a cuckoo nut.

'Err . . . it's the coconuts,' Inspector Abdul Rahman told her diplomatically, unsure how to put it without hurting the witch doctor's feelings, 'Are you sure they will work?'

'Eh, I'm not the only one using coconuts as magical tools, you know!' She defended her actions, irritated that they doubted her prowess when she was here to help them out. It was relatively an easy ritual, but as usual, clients made it hard for her with their disbelief.

'*You lupa eh?* Shamans of our calibre have been using coconuts since our *nenek moyang* days,' Bomoh Mona Mawar reminded the two men of the 2017 incident where a shaman conducted a beach ritual to ward off a supernatural attack from the netherworld with just two coconuts, a pair of sticks as binoculars, five bamboo cannons, a carpet, and a bowl of sea water. 'If coconuts can protect us from a hell-break, it can protect you two from Chang Pai Lian.'

'Th—That sounds ridiculous,' Ernest commented, flabbergasted that anyone would believe this mumbo jumbo. He was against coming here, but no, the inspector had insisted on it. Pai Lian had not done any harm to him. If there was anything at all, she was writing a book in his name . . . a potential bestseller by the looks of it, the first he would have after a failed career as a writer. Lest anyone forgot, she had saved him from suicide too.

'Ridiculous?!' Bomoh Mona Mawar snapped at Ernest's incredulity. She had a good mind to drop everything, probably with these coconuts at the feet of these goons for irritating her so. She thought they had wanted her help but here they were questioning everything she was doing and stressing her out. '*I tanya sikit.* Did you all suffer from hellish tribulations so far ah?' That would be a hard no. Had the magic worked? Or did the shaman get lucky?

'*Jawab I ni*, do you all want to do this or not?!' an irritated Bomoh Mona Mawar asked them directly to their faces, impatience clearly heard in her voice. It didn't matter to her if she lost this business opportunity as she had countless others who would beg for her services. '*Cakap saja* and we can end this,' she told them what was in her mind without mincing her words, not one bit.

'O . . . Okay,' Inspector Abdul Rahman relented with a sigh, uncomfortable at making a scene. God knows what she could do to them if aggravated further. It wasn't wise to invite the wrath of a witch doctor when you already had a ghost problem.

'We'll do what you say without any more questions,' he told Bomoh Mona Mawar apologetically, duly ashamed of the troubles they had caused. It was his idea in the first place, and the witch doctor came highly recommended, so it should be good, right? 'What do you want us to do with these coconuts?' he asked, a little curious what she would have them do.

'*Simpan* these coconuts with the evidence you want to protect. I've cast a spell of protection on them already,' she told Inspector Abdul Rahman, 'That'll protect *you punya barang*. To protect your persons, you need to *mandi bunga mawar.*'

'What did she say?' Ernest asked nervously before being told they had to take a rose flower bath. That wasn't so bad. Flower baths were quite common in this part of the world, basically to wash away evil misfortune and bad luck. However, it was the first time he had heard that it could be done for protection.

'I have the roses,' Bomoh Mona Mawar announced suddenly before sashaying to the vase and picking up two of the rose stalks that were in it. Ever so gingerly, she placed them into their hands; one stalk for the inspector and the other for Ernest before winking at them, 'I had a vision that you all would need these, hence my show-and-tell earlier.'

Have you ever died before?
Hell is more than six feet deep.
Endless nightmares at its core,
Hearing my dead sister weep.

Have you ever been to hell?
Where the stars don't shine.
How do I get there, pray tell?
To redeem this sister of mine.

Another night of mist, this time without the blood moon.
Another night of missing my twin sister, this time with
blood on my hands. I, Chang Pai Lian, should be the one
in hell, not her!

I was the one who sent her to her death with a pearl
necklace on her neck and now her neck was on the line
with hell to pay. I've got to do something, anything for my
Red Lotus! Her sins were mine to bear after all the hurt
I had caused my sister!

I was angry with my sister,
My heart went dark with fears,
Jealousy grew, hatred festered.
Day and night, I cried my tears.

Regret was remorse awaken,
Hell was me, living or dead,
My soul broken and shaken,
Now I go to hell in her stead.

I needed to break into hell to rescue my twin sister; I would kneel on broken glass at the feet of the Ten Yama Kings if I had to. By hook or by crook—in this case, burning hooks and crooked blades of the underworld—I would see my sister, Hong Lian, free from the suffering of hell even if it was the last thing I did. I couldn't even care less if heaven and hell forfeited my one and only chance at reincarnation. I didn't deserve one, not after what I had done.

Here I was, I had earned my ticket to hell so to speak in less than forty-nine days. Time was running out, and I needed to confess my sins in a book and drain my heart of my deepest regrets—writing my best, of my worst—warts and all. From here on out, it was a departure from my book *A Bridge to Murderville* that I had written for Adrian Holmes a long, long time ago.

Sorry, Adrian, I would have to put my sister, Hong Lian, first for she was right—blood is thicker than water, not that I didn't love you. She forgave me unconditionally, and I would reciprocate her kindness wholeheartedly by rescuing her soul from the pits of hell; assuming her sins were mine if I had to, for it was the least I could do, surely you would understand that.

In case, you didn't know, she forgave you, too, and wanted you free—her dying wish I would see fulfilled, I swore to all in heaven and hell.

Fortunately, your liberation, my sister's salvation, and my redemption all led to one person—Lady Nightshade, the psychic medium under the employ of your estranged wife, Marguerite Daisy. She would not make it easy for me, and quite frankly, I wouldn't expect her to.

The Key to Hell is in Lady Nightshade's hands,
A crystal pendant that'll take me to its gates.
The moon below will turn dark across the land,
Only then I can sneak in and challenge our fates.

The Key to Hell is in Lady Nightshade's defeat,
A battle will ensue with undying fear and dread.
Getting the crystal pendant will be no small feat,
But go I must, to where the angels fear to tread.

Killing three birds with a crystal pendant, that was my strategy, if truth be told. For starters, it would get me into hell where I would face Horse Face, which was what I needed to enact my action plans. And I had in mind some devious trickery up my sleeve to deal with this deity.

For Adrian Holmes' liberation, I had to procure the *fúchén* horsetail flywhisk called Cloud-Killer from Horse Face. It had the power to send devastating plagues of viruses across all realities—a flick from it could potentially send viruses into cyberspace, capable of hacking the evidence even if they had stored it in Cloud.

Once in hell, I would also have to make my way to Ox Head's chamber to liberate the *Niu Wang* bullwhip or more commonly referred to as the Ox King bullwhip. Yes, it was the same one that caused Hong Lian much grief the other time we encountered it. She needed it to fight us out of hell. If she did it successfully, she would have her salvation from hell and I, my redemption at last. That was the initial plan, a big IF from the looks of things. Plans could change along the way, of course, as I couldn't be certain of what would happen exactly when I was down there.

Just pray that we don't meet the Heibai Wuchang deities of impermanence, and we would be alright, I thought.

I knew it was silly, but I was desperate. There was no time to rethink my plan anyway as my forty-nine-day redemption period leeway would be gone in a blink of an eye if I weren't careful. Whatever problems I would face, I would cross the bridge when I came to it. With a wry sardonic laugh, I thought of how ironic it was that the writer of *A Bridge to Murderville* had to cross to the other side of hell where the worst of murderers and other condemned souls congregated.

Ding Dong, Ding Dong, went the doorbell urgently in the dead of the night. It was music to my ears; my target was at the door. I suddenly believed in the power of God, duly humbled by his infinite mercy for granting me a smooth passage to hell, well in due time of course.

'You had to set my appointment this late in the night?' Lady Nightshade complained aloud, glaring at the chiropractor, Kim Wang, the *tit-tar* bone-setting master, and giving him the evil eye of deep displeasure. Right off the bat, my first impression of her was bad already as she came off as an entitled, haughty Karen just because she was in the employ of the rich and famous Marguerite Daisy Holmes.

She looked nervous like she had seen a ghost, pacing up and down the medicinal hall while ranting at the same time, 'I didn't want to come. I read my horoscope and it was a horror story, says I would meet with an unexpected calamity and suffer a loss of property.'

That was a revelation. *You got that right, sister*, I laughed wickedly inside my heart, *you just wait*. I had been waiting for Lady Nightshade at her usual chiropractic shop in Istana Larut, Taiping. I hadn't gone through the trouble of possessing Kim Wang for the heck of it. Lady Nightshade was frazzled and bothered, just as I had planned. By tonight, I would have her crystal pendant, one way or another!

I had gone through great pains to set up this trap, tricking Lady Nightshade with a phone call asking her to postpone her follow-up appointment to a much later time . . . my time at night-time. She had to accommodate because her old bones had been acting up again. Hong Lian had really done a number on Lady Nightshade the other time, more than the stubborn psychic medium had cared to admit.

She really had no idea who she was dealing with, I noticed, all she saw was Kim Wang, when in actuality she was talking to me, not realizing that I had possessed him already. Devious trickery, yes, but what did she expect? I was a ghostwriter for a famous crime novelist, and I could out-think most people on devious plot set-ups and how to get away with murder if I wanted to.

'Come into Treatment Room #1,' I told Lady Nightshade, aware that my best-laid plans could still go awry because Lady Nightshade's psychic abilities could kick in at any time. But upon seeing her all worked up like that over the schedule change meant there was little chance of that happening since she had to be in a certain meditative state of mind for her psychic powers to work. *Ahh . . . the littlest details matter*, I reminded myself.

Yes, she was blind to my ruse for now, but I was taking no chances and proceeded to disarm her of any magical artefacts that she might have brought with her as protection. 'Strip off everything and wear the medical gown on the exam table,' I instructed her as I rolled a trolley cart of Chinese medical utensils and supplies next to her side.

The unwitting Lady Nightshade did as she was told, suspecting absolutely nothing while complaining to me where her body hurt. I pretended to care to keep up my pretences, silently nodding my head every now and then while examining her spine and joints, looking for any misalignment or tenderness.

'Strap up,' I said to her, and that was when she started getting a tad suspicious. There was an awkward pause before Lady Nightshade remarked, 'You never asked me to do that before.'

Then eyeing the silver-plated acupuncture set on the trolley cart, she casually asked me, her manner a little cold, 'What's with the needles?'

'The straps? Oh, I need to restrain you in a certain position before I realign your bones again,' I told her without batting an eyelid, trying to appear confident when I was nervous serving all that hogwash to her. I didn't want anything to go wrong at this point, not when was so much depended on me to make it right. 'As for the needles, I need to relieve the pressure points in your body so you'll feel less pain,' I reassured her gently, making it all up.

She sat still for a moment, appearing to be unsure, clearly contemplating on something while looking at me up and down before acquiescing to my directives. Without wasting a second, I strapped her up immediately before she could change her mind and decide to be difficult with me and jeopardize everything.

It was not a moment too soon when she realized that I had strapped her a little too tight and began to squirm. I almost wanted to laugh but didn't dare when I saw her eyes widening with fear as I brought out a hypodermic syringe.

'Wait, wait, wait! That's not an acupuncture needle!' she protested loudly, panic rising in her bile. She didn't need her sixth sense to tell her I was up to something. She started struggling and screaming before asking, 'What are you trying to do to me?'

She could scream all she wanted, it wouldn't do her any good, I had seen to that myself—it was night-time, and it was raining heavily due to the monsoon. Besides, it was a public holiday, and everyone was back in their hometown. *Too bad, sister.*

To be honest, I had wanted to put her at ease by going with the script and informing her that it was some Chinese herbal solution. It was anything but that—it was a potent truth serum of the narcosynthesis type, concocted with amobarbital, 3-quinuclidinyl benzilate, midazolam and thiopental to put her in a hypnotic state so she could be more liberal with her words.

'Let me go!' Lady Nightshade screamed as I injected the truth serum into her vein on her arm, and it wouldn't be long before she started singing like canary in a coal mine.

'Ooooo . . . give me more of those,' she cooed as her eyes started rolling sideways independent of each other in pure pleasure. She was so relaxed that she started singing nursery rhyme in reverse on the exam table. Kim Wang would be absolutely shocked if he heard this, I would imagine.

'Tell me . . . where is your crystal pendant, your Key to Hell?' I asked Lady Nightshade, eager to know where she had kept it. A precious treasure like that would have to be kept someplace secretive, away from prying eyes and thieving hands, a place no man would think of.

'Naughty, naughty you . . .' she giggled senselessly before mumbling incoherently, 'Why, it's in the darkest place of all, of course.' Then, out of the blue, she broke into a song, 'Where the sun doesn't shine, where the sun doesn't shine,' to the tune of an irritating instant noodle jingle from the sixties.

'Damn it! She is so out of it,' I thought, berating myself for using too potent of a truth serum and ruining everything. Then, it hit me. She was telling the truth—her Key to Hell hidden in the darkest place of all. She had kept it there, in her heart.

It made perfect sense to me. Her heart was evil and it had to be the darkest part of her being where the sun didn't shine. But as with all witches of Romani descent, she had kept it safe with a spell. I needed to know it before I could unlock her evil heart. What was the spell again?

'Where the sun doesn't shine, where the sun doesn't shine,' Lady Nightshade kept singing and humming that irritating instant noodle jingle again. I was about to ask her for the spell when I realized she had already given it to me. Thank you, truth serum! Thank you, Lady Nightshade!

The moment I sang the instant noodle jingle in tandem with Lady Nightshade, the Key to Hell crystal pendant started reforming outside her heart. I grabbed it without hesitation and fled from the scene as soon as I could, leaving Kim Wang's body unpossessed and slumping on the floor.

19

'What did you lose again?' a shocked Marguerite Daisy Holmes asked a distraught Lady Nightshade, disbelieving her ears when she was told that the psychic medium had lost the precious crystal pendant to a ghost through devious trickery. Even more unbelievable was the fact that this good-for-nothing sow had 'The Key to Hell' in the very first place. 'How the Devil did you get to possess a thing like that?'

Stung by Marguerite Daisy's insensitivity, Lady Nightshade's knee-jerk response was to retort *the devil had everything to do with it*, but her burst of tears stalled her tongue. Marguerite Daisy's choice of the word 'possess' crushed her totally, bringing to mind her shame for not recognizing a possession when she saw one, right in front of her eyes some more. Some psychic medium she was, Lady Nightshade berated herself mercilessly as she sobbed and sobbed with much regret.

'I—I stole it from Gerald, Kok Yu, and Wea Fung in Heavenly Eden a long time ago,' she managed to spill the beans in between sobs. 'I guess I was possessed by the Devil,' she surmised, which would explain her bravado for stealing from the rich and powerful. No wonder they all hated her and it was rather puzzling that they didn't try to steal it back from her—the legend of the curse surrounding the enchanted crystal pendant had something to do with it probably, if she were to hazard a guess.

How very interesting, Marguerite Daisy thought of this bunch of billionaires—she didn't quite peg them as adventurous collectors who were into Indiana Jones shit. But first things first, the shit was about to hit the fan judging from the disagreeable smell emanating from the goat carcass right in front of her.

'If you are going to perform a haruspicy ritual, please don't digress for goodness' sake,' Marguerite Daisy complained, unable to come to terms with the divination of sacrificial animals, being a patron and the face of PETA, an animal rights group, 'The stench is getting to me!'

It wasn't just the neighbours that she had to be worried about but the authorities to contend as well for breaking a health code. Worse still, there could be paparazzi lurking around and she loathed to have her pictures linked to what would look like a satanic ritual even though haruspicy was a different thing altogether.

From what she knew, haruspicy was even practiced by the Etruscans in ancient Italy and the Assyro-Babylonians, as well as the Romans, Greeks, and Vikings back in the old days—essentially it was the art of studying animal entrails that had unfortunately come to be associated with the dark arts.

'I found the *caput iocineris*,' Lady Nightshade declared triumphantly and lifted the head of the liver for Marguerite Daisy to see for herself. This essentially bode good omen and the psychic medium proceeded to inspect the visceral side of the liver, nodding and shaking her head as she went along, 'So far so good, your effort won't go kaput,' she quipped.

Next, the psychic medium dug her fingers into the stomach and found a half-ingested jasmine flower. She lifted the dead bloom to Marguerite Daisy and asked cryptically, 'Do you know of any Jasmine?'

'Why yes, as a matter of fact there is a Jasmine who happens to be Adrian Holmes' lawyer,' she replied with a mysterious smirk, 'I know just what to do.'

20

It was a busy morning for the officials at Taiping Prison when it came to visitation hours, but Jasmine Somasundram had it relatively easier than others on account that she was a lawyer from a big legal firm in Taiping. Before long, she was ushered into a meeting room to meet her client Adrian Holmes, who was sitting at a table, shackled wrists-to-feet while waiting for her.

'Good morning, Mr Holmes,' Jasmine greeted a very sullen Adrian as she placed her black briefcase onto the table while taking her seat in front of him. Obviously, the man didn't take too kindly to prison life, looking more like he was waiting for a runaway freight train to bust him out from here to Fantasy Island.

Don't fret, Jasmine secretly thought to herself, she didn't want to be here on a public holiday either when she could be in bed listening to Carnatic Indian classical music than all his jazz about not murdering Chang Hong Lian. The prosecutors had already established Adrian's ties to the vagrant . . . a somebody called Anthony Holmes, apparently his own brother from another mother, a recently deceased man found by the lotus lake at Taiping Botanical Garden.

That, on top of the purported confession of his, which was reportedly caught on a handphone camera of one of the night guards and had now gone viral. He was talking to a ghost it seemed . . . on his own volition. How could it be proved that his confession was under duress like that? How would one expunge the evidence on technical ground then? From where she was sitting, she was looking at a dead man walking on death row already. Unless . . . she turned it around creatively to their advantage.

'Good morning again, I bring you good news!' she told Adrian Holmes smiling brightly, preferring to start the meeting on a positive note. 'We are going with the insanity plea.' Well, that was one way to go about it. Who confessed everything to a ghost? Only a mad man did! The jury panel would lap it all up and the video was proof of Adrian's madness, what with him talking nonsense and all.

'Don't worry about my murder trial,' Adrian told Jasmine as he brightened a bit up somewhat, confident that Pai Lian would do what she needed to do to clear his name and get him out of Taiping Prison—a notion that his lawyer wasn't privy to at all. If he knew Pai Lian well, she would even exonerate him by undertaking all blame unto herself . . . she was such a fool for love. After all, she was already dead, and he wasn't. She was altruistic like that. 'It isn't my trial that I am worried about this time, but another thing that I wanted done as soon as possible,' he said.

'Not worried about your murder trial?! Hello, your very life depends on the outcome of this trial, for goodness' sake,' a perplexed Jasmine sputtered, shocked out of her senses. *Well, maybe the insanity plea was the right approach after all,* she thought, *when the man himself can't care less about his own life hanging in the balance!* Without missing a heartbeat, she faked through her response and continued, 'What is it that you needed done? Rest assured our firm will do it for you, sir.'

'Draw up divorce papers for me,' Adrian instructed Jasmine, smiling jubilantly now that he had made his bold move to save his $100 million fortune from his grubby wife's dirty hands. Deep inside, he knew his wife had reasons for divorce on grounds of his infidelity, but unfortunately for her, she did not have a single proof of that . . . her loss. Good thing too that both of his mistresses were dead already, so no living proof there.

Conjectures and hearsays wouldn't get her anywhere, not in a court of law. With the Lord as his witness, he wouldn't part with a single cent, let alone all of his massive fortune. 'I am divorcing Marguerite Daisy. Get it done quickly, it is a race against time!'

'Consider it done,' Jasmine declared, happy that the legal firm she was working for had another job from Adrian; a bonus would look so good right about now. Never mind the man was guiltier than the proverbial butler, as long as she made a killing off him, everyone would be happy, especially her bosses. 'Now, let's talk about your upcoming murder trial. We need to sort out a few key points,' she told Adrian while opening her black briefcase and taking out her documents for the latter's perusal.

A picture of an old lady slipped out and she halted for a moment, caught in a trance wrought by memories. There, in her hand was the picture of her beloved late grandmother, her *pãtti* in Tamil, the woman who saw her through university and got her where she was today.

'Which part of "get it done quickly" don't you understand?' Adrian rudely asked Jasmine, more eager to get the divorce proceedings rolling than his own murder trial. To him, he had everything more or less under control with Pai Lian around—it just wasn't what his lawyer was thinking or expecting. *Don't worry, everything has a way of working out, you'll see,* he reassured himself, *everyone would see it finally at the end, not my end!*

'Excuse me?!' Jasmine retorted as she slipped the picture back into her briefcase, appalled that Adrian didn't seem to care about his own impending murder trial seriously enough. How did the old Chinese saying go again? 'If the emperor wasn't worried but his eunuchs were . . .' Figuratively speaking, was it not? If Adrian wasn't worried, why should she be bothered, right? It wasn't like her own neck was on the line, Adrian's was. *Take a chill pill, angsty hangman,* Jasmine laughed inside her heart.

'Okay, we'll speak about it on another day at your earliest convenience. I'll get your divorce papers drawn up by then,' Jasmine told him diplomatically even though she wanted to slam the documents in his face, 'As you can see, we are working even on public holidays. Rest assured, we are committed to a favourable outcome for you, sir.'

'Yeah, yeah . . .' Adrian dismissed his lawyer with a lazy wave of his hand before being promptly accosted by the officials, who led him back to his holding cell, leaving a fuming Jasmine to rearrange and repack the legal documents back into her briefcase.

It sure looked like choo-choo train had left the station and was off to La La Land, Jasmine made a mental note to herself on Adrian's current state of mind, *that stupid bastard is so out of touch with reality,* she observed and almost felt sorry for him. Death row wasn't easy on anyone, especially on someone like him who was used to the high life.

'Where's the ladies' room?' she asked the guard as he opened the door to let her out. She wanted to relieve herself first before hitting the road, in case she got caught in a traffic jam later. Noting that the guard didn't say anything but merely pointed to a restroom sign at the corner of the hall, she didn't respond with a courtesy thank you either and just walked off towards the sign but halted midway when she saw Marguerite Daisy exiting from it.

What a coincidence, Jasmine thought and slowed down her pace to avoid bumping into Adrian's wife, or soon-to-be ex-wife to be exact. She didn't fancy having awkward chit-chat with Marguerite Daisy even though they knew each other socially at parties hosted by mutual friends. Only when Marguerite Daisy had disappear out of sight did Jasmine quicken her pace towards the restroom and disappear into the first stall she saw.

Phew, that was a close call, Jasmine sighed with huge relief as she dropped her knickers and relieved herself. How awkward would it be bumping into someone you were drawing up divorce papers for? Marguerite stood to lose a big fortune with this divorce and if she were Marguerite, she would give Adrian a hell of a fight.

Oh well, everyone knew Adrian fooled around but too bad Marguerite Daisy didn't have any proof of it, making their pre-nup a useless piece of document. If the latter did, Adrian would be the one to lose everything. *Maybe a motive like that was reason enough for Adrian to commit murder,* Jasmine surmised, *before Marguerite Daisy got the proof that she needed to take him to the cleaners.*

Too bad, Adrian has made his move to divorce Marguerite, Jasmine thought, feeling a little sorry for the wife as she cleaned herself up before hoisting up her knickers and flushing the toilet.

With a move like that, it was just a matter of time that Marguerite Daisy would be written out of his will as well, Jasmine knew, what would the woman do then with nothing to show for an ill-fated marriage?

'Poor, poor Marguerite Daisy,' Jasmine pitied the woman as she shook her head thinking about that poor woman's plight when something caught her eye—it was the precious South Sea double-stranded pearl necklace hanging on a utility hook on the toilet door . . . right in front of her . . . clearly belonging to Marguerite Daisy!

How the hell did she not notice this before? How the hell did someone misplace a precious piece of jewellery in a public toilet? 'Looks like Marguerite Daisy is now poorer by $50 million too, on top of the fortune she already stands to lose from her divorce,' Jasmine chuckled with glee at the poor woman's carelessness.

Should she run after Marguerite Daisy and return her pearl necklace? Or should she keep it—finders, keepers!

'Ooooo . . .' Jasmine cooed at the sheer magnificence of it as she caressed the masterpiece, tempted beyond reason to keep it for herself. It was calling her name, a voice in her head echoed seductively to her baser instincts, *it would look so good on me—a find of a lifetime, I am now rich, fifty million times over!*

Her heart said no, it didn't belong to her. She should do the right thing and return the pearl necklace back to Marguerite Daisy. If her *pãtti* were here, her venerable grandmother would tell her to ignore it, pick not a sen from the pavement for it could bring curses and bad luck.

The thought of her beloved grandmother momentarily shocked her back to reality and tears fell down her cheeks. Her pãtti would rather die in poverty tapping rubber trees for a living than take what didn't belong to her, God bless her soul.

Stories of cursed jewellery swirled in her mind—the Hope Diamond, the Delhi Purple Sapphire, the Black Prince's Ruby, the Koh-i-Noor Diamond, the Black Orlov—all came to her mind, causing her more confusion and undue distress. *No, no, no . . . you are not your grandmother*, the voice in her head told her, *you are a big-time lawyer, not some rubber tapper like your* pãtti!

'Sorry, pãtti, I can't live and die like you,' Jasmine apologized in her heart, sobbing profusely, having made her decision. She felt guilty that she was disobeying her grandmother, especially when the old woman had seen her through higher education with her own bare hands. 'I can't go on suffering under the likes of Adrian Holmes anymore, underappreciated and working through public holidays.'

With a heavy heart and a river of tears, Jasmine Somasundram placed the South Sea double-stranded pearl necklace onto her slender neck, locking shut the jewellery's elegant clasps with a feeling of finality and feeling herself hit a new rock bottom inside her soul before walking out of the ladies' room.

Then it happened all of a sudden—the drug addict apprehended by a policeman at the station thought he heard the pearls calling out to him—'kill me,' they said. With sheer hatred in his eyes, he glared at Jasmine as she walked towards the doors, anger rising in his blood without any apparent reason.

Time slowed to a blur as the ensuing events unfolded in quick succession—the drug addict snatched the hidden blade from his right boot and stabbed the startled policeman apprehending him in a deft move before lunging towards a screaming Jasmine, 'No . . .'

'Halt!' the policeman was heard yelling as he unwittingly shot into a packed room, causing further panic and mayhem as the bullet ricocheted across the room and hit a sleepy aquarium next to Jasmine—shattering it into a hundred pieces with the pressure of outflowing water showering her with shards of broken glass.

Luckily for Jasmine, her black briefcase protected her major organs although slivers of cuts were all over her arms and legs. Then, suddenly, the briefcase cover fell open and the picture of her pãtti, which she had kept inside for good luck, slipped out.

'Oh pãtti . . .' Jasmine cried, more in gratefulness than in pain, knowing who had saved her despite her disobedience. Her life was in peril and there was no time to wallow in regrets. She tried to get up despite her wounds but for some strange reason, she delayed standing up just yet, choosing to pick up the picture of her grandmother instead.

Her unwitting assailant beat Jasmine to it, standing up first instead of her and in his confused state of mind tried to make a run for it towards the doors. He didn't make it as a barrage of bullets ended his life before he could get out of the police station.

'Saved for the second time,' Jasmine realized, knowing deep in her heart that she could have ended up being hurt by a barrage of bullets had she stood up first. Danger was everywhere— somebody had wanted her dead, very likely Marguerite Daisy, she thought, for sending the cursed South Sea pearl necklace her way . . . probably to prevent her from drawing up the divorce papers.

In sheer panic and much distress, she cried to all in heaven for her pãtti to come save her. Then, a strange wave of reverie overwhelmed her as a sense of calm took over when she saw her grandmother at the end of a tunnel by the police station's doors.

'Come to me child,' the mirage of her pãtti beckoned to Jasmine with outstretched inviting arms. Without a moment's hesitation she stood up despite being in immense pain and ran towards her beloved grandmother, accidentally dropping the old lady's picture onto the dirty, messy floor in her hurry.

But something wasn't right, Jasmine ran and ran in an endless dark tunnel towards the light exuded by the mirage and realized her mistake only too late—in a split of a second, the familiar face of her pãtti changed to an unfamiliar one, that of a well-preserved English lady in white Chantilly lace, carrying a brolly with an intricate demonic bone handle.

Before Jasmine knew it, the blindingly white light of an oncoming bus hit her outside the police station, ending her life with a loud horrifying screech; her poor, broken body smashed into a thousand unrecognizable pieces with blood splattering everywhere.

'Oh, you were almost too troublesome to handle, my dear. You should have listened to your grandmother's advice,' Madam Petunia Yates remarked coolly, 'You really shouldn't be so covetous of other people's belongings. You don't deserve your grandmother's love one bit, you know that?'

Madam Petunia Yates had earlier made a bet with her beloved daughter, Marguerite Daisy, that she could take out the lawyer in three simple moves . . . which of course she did, much to her immense pleasure and pride.

'I can't wait to deal with Chang Pai Lian when she comes for the evidence,' she confessed rather haughtily. All the mother-and-daughter team needed to do was wait for the opportunity that would come sooner or later. Initially, there were two Chinese ghosts to deal with, but as of now, it was just one and that would make an easier job for her.

'Come one or come two, I don't really care,' Madam Petunia Yates yawned in a display of pure arrogance that wasn't out of character for a woman of her breeding and station, 'They have not met a formidable witch like me before.'

Humming her favourite tune 'Fair Petunia', she casually kicked away Jasmine's shattered head out of her way before leisurely walking inconspicuously into the crowd while breaking into her favourite song:

If I could dance like a singing star,
Up on a stage I call Fair Petunia back,
I'm crazy about my Fair Petunia, the only one I love,
Fair, fair, fair Petunia the only one I love,
Fair Petunia is sending me home to my grave.

21

Hell rises on the back of sins,
Bursting through the lies of life.
Burning souls crying up a din,
Demons damned to life of strife.

Using blades to stab our hearts,
Getting axe and cut us to parts.
Breaking sinners on their graves,
Giving us hell they clearly crave.

In hell, time is eternal. Endless torture plagued Hong Lian on endless nights, her karmic retribution damning her to the bitter end and beyond; the life she knew was gone like the ceremonial red candles they had placed on her altar during her wake, blown away by the wind and the rain. Wrecked with pain, she retreated further into her mind to escape the terrors of the night and the horrors of her plight until her sad, sad heart started breaking, decaying, and dying from sheer exhaustion of waiting for respite.

But mercifully, respite from the endless torture did come—the demons were too exhausted to go on and thankfully needed a break from breaking the multitude of condemned souls in this dark hell, hers included. This indistinct moment of brief respite was a welcome relief and the realization of demons taking their break soon permeated the oppressive darkness.

Alas! It was a false sense of respite, they knew, it would last only until the next time they looked into the horrifying soulless eyes of the demonic dead. Despite this, they took a deep breath and enjoyed the moment of reprieve from their sentences in hell. It wouldn't last for long, they knew, might as well enjoy it while they could.

'I regret my sins, have mercy on my soul,' a fallen goddess wailed, she who had traversed the earth at its dawn of birth when the sky clouds were just sporadic smoke vapours. Her sin? She had seen the dark universe yawning and wilfully killed the innocent child of the Night Deity and set the dark planets rolling into oblivion. She would be in hell for her terrible transgression . . . forever!

'I had plunged my spear into the heart of a deer in a primordial grove,' confessed a hunter who cried in pain and terror as he relived the horror of his sins, 'I threw its fawn to my pack of dogs to be torn into shreds.' A look at his disembowelled torso revealed his terrifying karmic retribution—his belly was in turn torn to bits by the fangs of the wolf packs from hell.

'I had plundered the royal tombs for ages, murdered a prince or two to usurp the throne,' confessed an old eunuch—chained by the bladed walls of hell as acidic drops of deadly poison dripped onto him and ate at his flesh. It was clear he had murdered using blades and poisons. For these sins of his, he wouldn't be released for another millennia or so.

'Oh great was my sin I had inflicted unto my soul,' Hong Lian lamented and sang her sorrow in a melodic Beijing opera fashion, startling one and all with her beautiful voice, akin to silver bells chiming in the breeze. 'I took my sister's lover and killed a witless homeless,' she sang of her regrets while tearing up with inconsolable emotions.

'So terrible are the sins of my spirit; so terrible is the reach of their doom,' she continued to regale one and all of her predicament. In between sobs and without missing a single beat, she lamented on her dire consequences, 'Now the pity of heaven can't atone me; now the wrath of hell fills my tomb.'

Hong Lian cried her heart out as applause reverberated across hell for her amazing singing skills. She looked up and smiled, bowing her head appreciatively at the impromptu audience and from the corner of her eyes, her furtive glances suddenly spied something very unusual.

Through the ghoul-guarded gateways of the dark hallways, past the abysses of torture chambers illuminated by the light of a waning moon, she saw that the demonic guards were fencing Granny Meng Po's broth.

From legends told throughout the ages, Granny Meng Po was the Goddess of Forgetfulness, serving in *Diyu*, the realm of the dead. She was tasked to prepare her magical broth for souls waiting to be reincarnated. A sip of it would bring about blessed forgetfulness, and the souls leaving *Diyu* would remember nothing of their time in hell to ease their trauma.

'Drink this up, forget your pain, leave your grief,' Hong Lian could read the gnarled lips of the ˙demon working for Granny Meng Po talking to its darkling friend, 'Drink this up, leave your haunting memories before they take a toll on you.'

Well, what do you know, demons could suffer from post-traumatic stress disorder too, Hong Lian realized, *just like the soldiers of war.* Inflicting hellish torture night in, night out over countless millennia would take a serious toll on any demon's mental health—true, not just humans but demons could be afflicted too. *No wonder demons were always nasty,* Hong Lian entertained the notion for a bit, *they have seen more hell than most.*

Break, Break, Break is over, back to hell,
Nothing has changed, bring on some pain.
Die, Die, Die, cower back into your shell,
Death will come, your blood in the drain.

The demon responsible for Hong Lian's torture came back with a bowl of Granny Meng Po's magical broth, his bitter tears of unhappiness had disappeared from his cheeks, replaced with a happy grin from ear to ear. His trembling claws holding the bowl belied his excitement, he was eager to consume its contents right away to ease his ravaging stress and pain.

Tap-tap-tippity-tap-tap, he traipsed along the uneven floor, careful not to spill a single drop of the precious broth—his eyes focusing on the bowl rather than looking where he was going. Oh, if only the path was cleared of rattling chains, walking would be such a breeze. Unfortunately, his gangly legs kept trembling from anticipation while his mind was mired in a deep haze just thinking about the mind-blowing release it would get from drinking the broth.

'Give me that, I beg of you!' the fallen goddess yelled and grabbed at the bowl of broth. She had been in hell for far too long already and she needed release more than the demon that inflicted torture on her, she reckoned. Unfortunately, the demon was far too quick for her and averted her grasp in the nick of time.

'You will pay for this effrontery,' the demon hissed angrily and hopped up into mid-air giving her a flying kick on her face, shattering all her pearly whites and breaking her nose. Goddess or not, all sinners had to learn their places in hell. Rebellion would not be tolerated, and she would be severely punished for the errors of her way.

'I want it too, I need it more!' the deer hunter screamed in a manic frustration, eager for the release that forgetfulness would bring. He knew there was hell to pay, but what had he got to lose? He was in hell already, screw the consequences he thought. With a swift move, he punched the demon right in the face and grabbed the bowl of broth as it fell from his grasp. Incredibly, not a single drop of the magical broth was spilled.

The deer hunter was about to sip the precious broth but was thwarted by a vicious kick from the demon, his lips missing a taste at the last moment. Sometime during the skirmish, the bowl of broth went flying upwards in a few deft moves, but the demon caught the bowl expertly as it came down and landed on the palm of his right hand.

Phew! That was close, the demon sighed a breath of relief. He glared at the deer hunter and gingerly placed the bowl of broth onto the floor and proceeded to torture him—whipping him with his own entrails and stringing him up with intestines as a bloody lesson to all. 'A punishment befitting his crime', the demon growled aloud, pleased with his handiwork.

As he turned to pick up his bowl of broth, the demon realized that the precious item had gone missing—the culprit could only be the eunuch or Hong Lian. Enraged, he roared and belted his cries of frustration deep from his belly, with flames bursting from his skin in a display of terrible anger. 'Who stole my broth?' he thundered!

Blinking rapidly with a vacant expression, both the eunuch and Hong Lian pointed at each other nervously. *Ahh, a mystery right here*, the demon thought, only one could do it but the question was who? The eunuch was extremely cunning; he had murdered princes and looted tombs. On the other hand, the girl, Hong Lian, was a fool for love although she had murdered a dim-witted homeless vagrant. *Who could it be?*

'You! The one who looted tombs, you must be the one!' the demon deduced. A thief would always be a thief as a leopard could never change its spots. That adulteress had taken a life sure, but it was no challenge by virtue that her victim was a homeless idiot. 'Give it back or you pay for the consequences!'

With the threat issued and without waiting for a reply, the demon grabbed the eunuch by the throat and held him up— and the demon was right—the precious bowl of broth slipped out of the long sleeves of his ceremonial robe but was caught in time by the quick reflexes of the demon. Without mercy, he crushed the windpipe of the eunuch, planning to add a list of new punishments just to teach this errant fool a lesson he would never forget.

Applause erupted across the crowds in hell—that was an impressive display of martial and acrobatic skills that this particular demon had demonstrated. It pleased the demon very much that everyone had witnessed his glory. As pride got into his big head, he broke into a victory dance before picking up his prized bowl of broth and blew the hot steam emanating from the broth.

As fate would have it, he didn't notice Hong Lian's long chains on the floor and accidentally tripped on it, causing him to fall and splash the entire bowl of broth onto the girl's dress!

'NO . . .' he hollered in pure anguish at his loss; his cries of dismay could be felt reverberating on earth, triggering volcanos that erupted on some Indonesian and Japanese islands in the Pacific.

How did the saying go again? Yes, this time Pride did come before a fall.

PART 3

The Showdown!

Over to the Naihe Bridge

22

It was not even a week that Inspector Abdul Rahman and Ernest Maxwell Graves had paid a visit to Bomoh Mona Mawar that the rotund Inspector came to see her again—this time with a bunch of red roses that bore the witch doctor's namesake. The kind florist had even painstakingly adorned miniature roses like Snow Brides, Apricot Drifts, and Deja Blu as side blooms to complement the larger main ones. Like a nervous teenager, there he was, standing at her door.

'Assalamu alaikum,' he hollered his greeting and wondered what he would say to her when he met her, coughing and clearing his throat while desperately trying to come up with a plausible excuse on why he had wanted to see her—Valentine's Day won't happen until February 14 and Malays typically didn't celebrate the occasion. But the fact remained that he was still very much under the influence of her love potion that he had unwittingly ingested the last time he and Ernest were here.

But today's visit wasn't about that, it was more about yesterday's dream—he was dead scared that he had foreseen his death during a showdown, and he needed her services to overturn this eventuality. While it was just a nightmare, he didn't want to take chances as it could be an omen from Heaven itself.

'Walaikum salam,' Bomoh Mona Mawar replied before opening her ornate main doors, and upon seeing him with a bouquet of red roses and the accompanying miniature blooms, her face lit up with joy. '*Terima kasih*,' she thanked the inspector, giggling with much pleasure like a teenage schoolgirl.

Pleased that Bomoh Mona Mawar loved the roses, Inspector Abdul Rahman beamed with joy, his face as red as the roses he had bought, feeling the butterflies in his stomach dancing with happiness. He didn't know how to broach the subject of needing her supernatural services for something as silly as a nightmare. He was an inspector for goodness' sake, losing his manhood over a nightmare that could probably be nothing. What would people say? *Tak jantan pun ini inspector, they would say questioning my manhood*, he imagined, feeling emasculated by his irrational fear.

Oh, this is all a terrible mistake, he thought, wanting to chicken out lest he be ridiculed. Oh the utter shame of it! Awkward didn't quite describe how he felt—he was at a total loss for words, stammering like an idiot with an aneurysm. He felt like a clown standing there and if there was a *sarkas* in town, he would run away with it for sure.

Choking with embarrassment, he suddenly burst into a bout of uncontrollable coughing, which startled Bomoh Mona Mawar and she jumped slightly backwards. There was something in his mind, she deduced, and from the looks of it, she sensed it had something to do with a dream that he was ill at ease to share.

'Come, come . . . You need a glass of water,' Bomoh Mona Mawar said gently before ushering Inspector Abdul Rahman into her luxurious abode, afraid that her neighbours would see this. 'You can tell me all about it, no worries. I can help! Sit right here while I get the antidote that you need,' she said and offered him a seat on her plush, gilded *Datin* sofa by the glass coffee table before disappearing into her kitchen at the back of her house to get a glass of water. 'I won't be long,' she reassured him before dashing into the kitchen.

Inside her kitchen, she hurriedly switched on the lights and opened her meranti larder to get a big glass mug and poured water from a kettle lying on her gas stove. With the glass full, she dashed outside to her living room and passed it to the Inspector to drink. *Glug, glug, glug* . . . it went down his throat, soothing him and halting the coughing spate.

'Feeling better?' she asked the Inspector and he nodded, feeling more relaxed after having finished half the water in the big glass mug. He placed it on the glass coffee table and dabbed his mouth.

'Why don't you tell me what you need?' she asked him on a serious note, 'Is it about your nightmare?'

'H—How did you know?' he asked her, a little shocked she had sussed out the reason for his visit. This Bomoh Mona Mawar might look like a joke to some people who thought she was a fraudster with parlour tricks, but her clients begged to differ. She did have something extraordinary in her; she had proved it the last time he was here with Ernest. 'I . . . I dreamt I died in a showdown with malevolent spirits. I don't want to die . . .' he admitted to her.

'It can't be a coincidence that I dreamt it too,' Bomoh Mona Mawar revealed to him before taking his hand and pouring the glass of remaining water on it, shocking him with the deliberate act—the water sieved between his fingers and splashed onto the glass coffee table—forming disparate images on it that she could decipher with her mind's eye as her own turned white.

'I'm afraid it wasn't just a nightmare, it was an omen as seen through my vision,' she declared as her white eyes scrutinized the images—on, between, and below the reflective surfaces of her glass coffee table, reading the shapes of the splashed water in all their perspectives simultaneously. As her eyes slowly reverted to normalcy, tears started flowing down her cheeks; the act of giving the unwitting inspector her love potion that day had bonded their hearts and souls together. If he died during the showdown, so would she. *What was she to do now*, Bomoh Mona Mawar fretted anxiously.

'Listen to me! Do *not* accompany Ernest and Pai Lian during the showdown with their enemies,' Bomoh Mona Mawar warned

Inspector Abdul Rahman vehemently, worried that he would have to do it in his capacity as the officer of law. 'You won't survive it!' she warned him again, 'But if you have to, join the fray only during the aftermath, faham?'

As Inspector Abdul Rahman fidgeted about nervously at her revelation, Bomoh Mona Mawar contemplated on what to do next. A life fated to be ended there would have to perish there in accordance with the Universal Law, destiny will not be cheated of a soul! But she could save him, she knew if she took his place in the fray. Was this God's will? To test the strength of her love potion? Or was this to test the strength of her humanity? Would she sacrifice for love, should she? *Is this how God has planned it*, she wondered?

In all honesty, Bomoh Mona Mawar knew she had a better chance at survival than Inspector Abdul Rahman when dealing with a threat like that. At least she had supernatural skills, unlike the man. This kind of threat was bigger than all of them had imagined. And by the grace of God, she had an opportunity to partake in what would be the first battle of the apocalyptic war.

For a very brief moment, she reasoned with herself on the odds—she would die if he died anyway . . . and his death was a certainty! However, if she died during the battle, at least his life would be safe and her sacrifice would be something meaningful in the eyes of God, she knew. Self-preservation did cross her mind, but for some strange reason, her life didn't seem all that important to her anymore. She was the one who gave the love potion to the Inspector and in a twist of fate, she was beginning to feel the effects of . . . love, oh merciful God!

'*Sudah ditakdirkan*, God's will, this is,' Bomoh Mona Mawar sighed in resignation and said to Inspector Abdul Rahman, 'Tell Ernest to prepare for the epic showdown. He and his ghost, Pai Lian, will be going to war, as will I.'

23

A dream, a sad, sad dream. Ernest Maxwell Graves screamed aloud in a void of darkness wrought by restless sleep. It was just a bad dream, a terrible nightmare—Chang Hong Lian being tortured body and soul in the deepest part of hell for her sins. A special kind of hell that taunted souls in the shadows of bitterness and dread; sinister and haunting until all hope was lost, along with faith and love.

Chained and shackled, the Red Lotus ghost was burnt to death while she was still alive, a thousand times over and over again with her beloved paper-and-bamboo effigies used for fuel. It was a fiery scene reminiscent of Chinese funeral pyres, only this time it was hers. Her soul was cruelly set ablaze while her hollow screams echoed into the endless night, feeding fear into the nightmares of other souls trapped in hell.

The dark red sky wept with bloody tears as she cried out in excruciating pain while the flames ate away at her flesh to the bone like they would a paper effigy to its bamboo core. No mercy was given, only endless misery and all her cries of pain fell on deaf ears.

In hell no one can hear you scream,
Cry inside your heart, scream aloud.
In hell, you die with all your dreams,
Dry your eyes, for crying out loud.

And then, after a very long unhurried nightmare, Ernest's dream was flooded by a beacon of light wrought by restful sleep; the nightmare eventually turned into a beautiful dream that calmed his nerves—it was Chang Pai Lian coming to her twin sister's rescue. Her love for her sister would lead the way, her heart following the latter's cries deep into the embrace of hell.

In a single burst of hope, white lotuses rained down from heaven, dousing the fires that plagued the Red Lotus ghost. Each bloom burnt by the hellfire was a torture to the White Lotus ghost who winced in pain having flown down from above to hug her sister, sharing in the pain in an effort to protect her. Her tears fought with the fury of the flames, moving heaven and hell to tears.

> Great pain, terrible pain I must endure,
> I weep, I cry, I plead, I try . . .
> Retribution is a lesson, love is the cure,
> I repent, I sacrifice, I die, I cry . . .

He tossed and turned in his sleep as a vision started unfolding in the dreamscape of his mind.

His eyes started moving rapidly under his eyelids, his breaths became raspy and his pulses raced across his body when a succession of mysterious images flashed before him.

The Key to Hell crystal pendant. A brolly with a bone for a handle. A magician's wand. A double-stranded South Sea pearl necklace. All of them didn't make an iota of sense to him until a strange poem with four-line stanza reverberated in his mind, and with it came some vague knowing.

> The Key to Hell will unlock gates, changing fates;
> More than glitter will come from your wand.
> The string of pearls will cause grief, stirring hate;
> Make the exchange, for mercy is now at hand.

'Oh no, no, no . . .' Ernest protested and jolted up from his sleep, caught totally unaware of what Pai Lian was about to do—break into hell to free her beloved sister, whom she had wronged by hook or by crook, using the stolen Key to Hell, no less, an enchanted crystal pendant that no God, devil, or deity would deem to touch. *Oh no, what have you done, my friend? How will I save your soul now?*

He tried to get up, which took a lot effort, and felt rather vulnerable as he sat on the edge of his bed and wept, his clothes drenched in sweat and tears. He was overwhelmed with anxiety, and his fists unconsciously clenched with stress as he walked nervously towards the big window in his hotel room to draw the heavy curtains and let the light in.

Mired in the warm kiss of the morning sun, he took a deep reassuring breath to ease the stifling suffocation he was feeling inside. Was his hotel room closing in on him or was it just him feeling a little bit under the weather today? All he knew was that he was invariably afraid to lose someone who had actually been good to him, and that he was worried sick he would somehow lose this friendship forever.

Come what may, he vowed to save Pai Lian's soul like she had saved his life.

I fly to the reversed world below,
In a blink of a thought, full of ease.
It feels like death, this hell I know,
Dissolution of souls is all I see.

The moon turns dark, my sin glows,
Alas! My inner demons lie in wait.
A rush of wind blows, blood flows,
Gates of hell open, my soul is bait.

Who rushed headlong into hell if not I, Chang Pai Lian?
I stood there hovering in its rancid air, a lone soul with
a glowing crystal pendant, looking beatified yet damned
for all the wrong reasons. The demons of hell had a
long memory, and from what they could recall in recent
centuries, I wasn't the only one who had ventured into
the netherworld.

There were tales of Mulian or Moggallāna if you
will, who saved his mother from hell with the help of
the Buddha. Others included Sāriputta, Jaratkaru,
Maudgalyayana to name but a few. Greek legends were
also full of them—mortals who had journeyed into Hades
like Orpheus, Odysseus, Heracles, Theseus, and many
others. Even the Thais had Phra Malai, the Buddhist
saint known for his legendary travels to heaven and hell.

There was this 'Taoist Tour to Hell' where you could visit the dead, too, but you had to undergo the Guan Luo Yin rituals and invoke the three Aunties—or the three Fates to some—for actual help in navigating the region. Apparently, you could explore hell, take up spirit world tour, meet the spirits and so on, but I digressed.

If anyone knew me at all, I was not really the type to subject myself to complicated rituals to go to the netherworld. My way was simpler—I stole the Key to Hell crystal pendant that would allow me to go down to the netherworld. I was sorry, but Lady Nightshade was just a convenient means to achieve my end. And here I was, hovering in the realm of hell, trying to liberate my sister, Chang Hong Lian.

Whatever would happen, would happen. I would deal with it when I cross the bridge.

I drew first blood: the Tengu demons—half man, half crow entities, well versed in martial arts—flew up to slay me but got thwarted by my crystal pendant. In a hurry, they didn't account for the reverse powers of my weapon, and it did more than throw them off-balance—it threw them off-world onto the earth of the living, which came as a shock to them as they struggled with disorientation.

The Belu ogres were a different story. These vampires looked exactly like humans but had red eyes and the inability to cast shadows, all cursed with sharp fangs and a corrosive touch. They lunged at me only to realize that I could teleport out of their reach easily. Hello? Which part of my teleporting to hell did they not get? If I could teleport long distance to hell, I could very well do short bursts of instantaneous travel within hell too.

War, war . . . the song of slaughter in hell,
Demons marching to drums of bones.
Die, die . . . your rotten soul is ours to fell,
All you've ever known will now be gone.

Legions of demons, ghouls, and darklings came forth singing their hearts out, if they had one in the first place, eager to damn me into hell and feast upon my soul. Their numbers got me running and I tried to escape from their arsenal of hellish weaponry, their relentless onslaught, as well as their gruesome flesh-eating maggots and slithering worms that were rippling and festering under their skin.

Like lightning, a BaShe serpentine demon capable of swallowing elephants whipped me with its tail, sending me crashing to the ground and getting me trapped in a corner. A greedy demon by nature, it wanted to swallow me whole and slammed both of its poisonous fangs at me, but they got caught in the walls instead.

Without any prompting, my crystal pendant reacted in defence, sending out a flash of white light that teleported the serpentine demon to its death into the heart of the sun, leaving behind two fangs still stuck on the walls. Instinctively, I plucked one out and used it as a weapon.

'T . . . This is not what I want, I don't want to take any lives,' I reminded myself, worried sick that the Kings of Hell would take it against me, which would put my plans in peril, 'Please stop, I beg of you.'

'Die, die . . . a terrible death,' a Huli Jing fox spirit somersaulted towards me and slashed me with her claws, but before she could effectively end me, she was teleported into the heart of a frozen moon, forever entombed in its cold embrace.

'No . . .' I wailed deep inside my heart, for I knew I couldn't afford hell's reprisals with the mounting death toll. Every corner I teleported to, dark shadows tried pouncing on me, haunting me with their unholy cries and eager to sever my head from my neck to satiate their darkest desires.

To make matters worse, the BaShe fang in my hand suddenly disappeared by will of God, leaving me weaponless with only my crystal pendant for protection.

Stop, stop . . . this dance of war in hell,
I come marching with tributes on pile.
Peace, peace . . . trust me all will be well
Free my sister, it'll be worth your while.

'What tributes are you talking about, Chang Pai Lian?' Ox Head bellowed at me as he and his partner, Horse Face, made their grand entrance, flanked by even more soldiers from hell, all flashing their sabres, spears, tridents, maces, crossbows, and rope darts—the fearsome dark brigade from the Valley of Death ready to do battle with me.

Shackled with burning chains was my sister, Chang Hong Lian, by the deity's feet, a broken doll of a woman having fallen into hell for her sins. She looked dazed and confused at first, but her face lit up with joy when she recognized me. 'Sister!' she hollered for my attention, teary-eyed.

My teardrops fell like petals in the wind, falling onto the unhallowed ground that all of hell lapped up hungrily. The blood of her grief tortured me beyond my sanity and caused me great pain and trepidation.

Run, run . . . I wanted to scream at her, but I knew it would do her no good. I wanted to charge in and push away the crowds, but I knew my rage would only fuel the cruel demons' lust for death—mine and hers. 'Sister,' I hollered back to console her, my heart broken at her plight.

Her sobbing echoed hopelessness, her tears a mournful cadence like the toll of a broken bell wrapped in sundering darkness. I was the cause of this, I was the sin she committed; I was the pain she had to endure, all this hell because of me!

'You heard him, what tributes are you talking about?' Horse Face reiterated Ox Head's question to me, curious as to what I could offer to secure the release of my beloved sister. It piqued his curiosity—no one had done this in eons, for none would enter a burning house to save a condemned soul, but I sure did.

"This crystal pendant—the Key to Hell,' I offered the deities, knowing it was what they wanted. In the hands of a lost soul like me, I could travel back and forth between earth and hell. In the hands of a deity, however, it could potentially take hell to earth or vice versa. It was a weapon of a dark god constructed solely to instigate Armageddon on earth and the ten Yama Kings of Hell would want it secured for the Jade Emperor, I was sure.

'But those who stole it are cursed to be condemned in hell forever, even the god who created this refused to touch it,' Ox Head told me, hinting of the terrible consequences awaiting me because I had stolen it from Lady Nightshade. 'Why do you think no one went stealing and killing for it?' he continued to ask.

'Ahh . . . I did just that, so you didn't have to,' I replied to Ox Head, smiling now that I got his full attention. 'I am *giving* it to you . . . in exchange for my sister.'

Of course both Ox Head and Horse Face knew how to read between the lines. If they killed me and stole it from my hands, they would be cursed to be in hell forever. Not even the deities of hell wanted to be in the netherworld for eternity once their stints of service to hell were over.

I got this insight from a Greek legend. Stories had it that Hades himself was pissed at Zeus and Poseidon for relegating him to rule in hell. Well, even the king of hell wanted out, what more could we say of those trapped in here?

'One doesn't simply walk in here and demand a soul to be released from hell,' Horse Face reminded me, neighing at my foolishness for breaking into hell. It was one heavenly law that had remained steadfast in its implementation. Only a few had managed to do so, some based on their own merits while others had the help they needed from higher form of beings.

'Ahh . . . but I am not alive, I am a ghost,' I reminded the deity politely, having thought this through long and hard. Heck, didn't they make exemptions on All Souls' Day? 'Besides, souls get released all the time during Hungry Ghost Festivals, do they not?' I asked him.

Well, that was one way to argue, and judging from their body language, they were buying it. Hell, why not? They would get a powerful weapon without having to break any precious heavenly rules, delivered straight into their hands.

From where I stood, I saw Ox Head and Horse Face were conferring with each other on their decision while referring to the registry of condemned souls every now and then. They nodded and muttered something that was inaudible to me.

'It is heaven's will,' Horse Face declared to all and sundry in hell, while Ox Head looked a little pensive for my liking at the revelation. Perhaps he didn't like the idea of releasing a condemned soul under any circumstances. 'Hong Lian's name has been struck off from the registry for now and she is free to go with you.'

Heaven's will?! Suddenly I knew what happiness was. It was heaven's blessing, even when we were dying in hell. It was wishes granted when we least expected them. Both Hong Lian and I broke into tears of joy, humbled by heaven's mercy in our hours of despair.

Happiness is seeing my sister free
Happiness is escaping hell together
Happiness is not being alone
Happiness is family to me

'Hand over the Key to Hell,' Ox Head commanded and I obliged, passing the enchanted artefact directly into his hands. With great sadness, he revealed to us the terms of our freedom, 'Just so you know, you have secured a respite from hell . . . for another forty-nine days.'

'We'll see each other again when your time is up,' Horse Face said to us, reminding us of our redemption period. Oh, great was the sin of our spirits, doomed to suffer in hell again, I lamented. 'A word of advice, use whatever time you have left wisely. Heaven is watching,' Horse Face advised us.

Before we knew it, Hong Lian and I were teleported back to our realm, courtesy of Ox Head who facilitated our transfer back to the real world. It was the last time we ever saw the crystal pendant, but for mankind, never again would they ever lay eyes on it.

24

30 December 1979

'Two ghosts?!' Inspector Abdul Rahman exclaimed, his voice tinged with so much fear that Ernest Maxwell Graves could almost smell the sweat in it. In his quivering fat hands were photocopies of Chang Pai Lian's latest chapter of the manuscript that told the story of how she freed her sister, Chang Hong Lian, from hell—frightening events that bordered on the fantastical that only fuelled the inspector's fear twice over.

'W . . . Where are the coconuts? We need the coconuts from Bomoh Mona Mawar like now!' he said, on the verge of having a nervous breakdown and grasping at straws while drowning in dread and distress.

'They are in my hands as you can see, so chill for a bit, will you?' Ernest told him, trying to calm the rotund man while wondering if the air conditioner was working properly because it felt a tad too warm in the server room of the Taiping Police Station. *Better crank it up before the fat man gets crankier,* he quipped to himself. 'Are you sure these coconuts will work? I am not so sure they will,' Ernest said.

Earlier that evening, they had met outside the annex building of the police station that was housing the main computing systems while waiting for the tech team to leave for the day—the Inspector needed to be inconspicuous, and Ernest understood why. Not only would it be embarrassing for an inspector to be caught with two coconuts, it would also be difficult to explain why a man of his stature still believed in the supernatural.

But believe in Bomoh Mona Mawar, the Inspector did. The witch doctor had asked him to place both coconuts close to where he kept the evidence of Adrian Holmes' confession in order to protect it from the ghost's interference—that he would do, desperate man that he was.

Only when the tech team called it a day did Inspector Abdul Rahman and Ernest felt comfortable enough to make their way inside the server room.

'They will work! They must, otherwise we are doomed, and I don't want to meet my maker today if that's alright with you,' Inspector Abdul Rahman hissed, more than a little irritated, and just wanting to get things done and over with.

That is easy for him to say, Ernest complained in his heart as he himself had a much harder time with all this than the inspector did—the man had no idea what it was like living with ghosts, oh for goodness' sake!

Worse still, the witch doctor had secretly slipped a bottle of love potion into his pocket—which had accidentally fallen and cracked open sometime last night. He still couldn't wrap his head around how that happened, but it had been unnerving waking up to see two beautiful ghosts staring at him, looking and feeling confused.

Both the Chang sisters had gone to hell and back over a man, and now this. The last thing he wanted was to be the centre of their attention, he shuddered.

'Let's bury the coconuts in pots and decorate them with plastic plants,' Inspector Abdul Rahman suggested to Ernest. It would be their secret; magical charms cleverly camouflaged and concealed, hidden in plain sight, none would be the wiser. 'That would work like a charm, wouldn't it?' he said and winked at Ernest, hoping to elicit some compliments from the man for his idea, but Ernest only rolled his eyes and groaned.

Then, out of the blue, the lights flickered and went out with darkness caving in like the world had died. Both men felt the impalpable impression of a presence floating eerily in the air before them as goosebumps riddled their arms and their heartbeats raised in alarm.

'W . . . Who's there?' Ernest stammered in fright, his eyes trying to focus on the apparition moving unsurely at the edge of his vision. Both he and the Inspector had the distinct feeling that someone's unearthly eyes were fixed on them and while they couldn't see her smile, they could unnervingly feel it. 'Chang Pai Lian?' Ernest asked timidly.

'No . . . it is me, Chang Hong Lian, her twin,' the apparition said and made her presence known, all dressed in a red stage costume of a Beijing opera diva while carrying a mysterious bowl of broth in her hands. She gave them a sad smile knowing they would rather be miles away than face her. But she had to do what they would *not* have her do.

'Gentlemen, give me your sympathy in my time of need,' she begged them while knowing it was already futile. What did they know about love? What did they know about sacrifices? 'I am here to extend my mercy to my lover who did me wrong,' she said and sobbed mournfully before breaking into an impromptu song and dance like she was on the stage, raising eyebrows and goosebumps even more.

> In my loving you, I come alive,
> But you killed our love, you killed me.
> Mercy I give you, so you will live,
> My love is true, I cry without shame.

'You still want to prove your love when he wasn't worth your tears,' Ernest told Hong Lian, exasperated at her misplaced passion and heartbroken at her plight. That Adrian Holmes had killed her and her baby, there was no coming back from that.

What was wrong with her? Her heart was badly hit by love, but did something hit her head too? 'You don't need him, and the world doesn't either.'

'I have to ask you to stop right there,' Inspector Abdul Rahman insisted, although he knew he had a ghost of a chance making his instruction stick, but he was still the authority here, damn it. Embolden by two coconuts, he suddenly grew a pair and told Hong Lian right to her face, 'Lady, I advise you to let the law take its course. Interfering with evidence is a felony.'

'Don't worry, I have it all worked out,' Hong Lian replied to the Inspector with a smile, a little amused that he would stand up to her when she clearly had the upper hand. What could his bullets do to her? They would just whizz right through her.

'With Granny Meng Po's Broth of Oblivion spilled onto the server, it would erase the evidence and the world will forget about it,' Hong Lian revealed what she had in the bowl she was carrying, 'With a drop of it onto your tongue, you won't even remember this unfortunate incident.'

Granny Meng Po? Wasn't she the goddess of forgetfulness tasked to erase the memories of inmates in hell who were crossing the Naihe Bridge to be reborn? What now, it also erased computer memory, was that it, Ernest wondered?

That doesn't even make frigging sense, Inspector Abdul Rahman thought to himself, struggling to wrap his mind around the idea until he recalled the movie *Matrix. What, this reality isn't real? What then, a simulation of sorts, is that it?*

Whatever it was, he got a massive headache just thinking about this nonsense. He hated the supernatural with a vengeance, give him scientific proof any day. But it did beg the question, how the hell did Hong Lian smuggle it up here?

As if in answer to that, Hong Lian explained while sobbing profusely, 'I was in hell and I suffered terribly beyond words. Unbeknown to me, the demons suffered greatly too and took solace in Granny Meng Po's Broth of Oblivion to forget their cruelty on the inmates, such extreme was our suffering that even the demons wanted to forget it all.'

In hell, there was no respite,
For both sinners and demons alike.
Cruelty, fire, torture, out of spite,
Forget the pain, we would like.

'A demon stole a bowl of broth from Granny Meng Po's kitchen to ease its mental torture,' Hong Lian recounted her story to us, sobbing as she spoke, 'As fate would have it, the demon accidentally tripped onto my chains and spilled the broth on my dress.'

Unheard of! Inspector Abdul Rahman scoffed at what he perceived as pure, utter nonsense. *Demons suffering from post-traumatic stress disorder? Only humans suffer PTSD having seen the hell on battlefields*, he grudgingly thought to himself.

'At first, I didn't think much of it as events unfolded too fast for me to dwell on it,' Hong Lian admitted, what with her sister, Pai Lian, coming to her rescue and the ensuing scuffle in hell and all, 'Only when I got back into the human realm did I realize I could wring the broth out of my soaked dress and into a bowl.'

Then, her tears flowed freely again, this time out of guilt. She had told Pai Lian that her love for Adrian Holmes had died on the day he killed her and her baby. And here she was, still trying to save him out of love.

I tried not to love you, tried finding other joys in life instead; yet you stuck around in my heart and mind, Hong Lian lamented and cried at her failure to fall out of love.

'It's not your fault, you couldn't help it,' Ernest said aloud having put one and one together, startling them with a shocking epiphany. Hong Lian was obviously bewitched by that love potion, which was possibly triggered by the presence of the two ghosts! 'You are under the influence of Bomoh Mona Mawar's love spell!'

'What is the point of making me love Adrian Holmes when I shouldn't?' a bewildered Hong Lian asked, overwhelmed with anguish by the realization that it was all an induced passion due to a love potion.

Am I really supposed to be here? Should I be doing what I am doing? She thought for a little while but couldn't come up with an answer. *The universe sure works in mysterious ways!* she concluded.

'There is a reason for all this, I am sure!' Inspector Abdul Rahman assured them, even though he was baffled as to why had Bomoh Mona Mawar slipped a love potion into Ernest's pocket. *Why did providence drive the Red Lotus ghost to come here?*

'What should we do now?' he asked everyone, man and ghost.

'Well, die of course!' a voice interrupted their conversation, as another formidable ghost made her entrance—this time belonging to a well-preserved English lady in Chantilly lace, armed with a brolly crafted from a demonic bone for a handle. 'Call me Madam Petunia Yates. Remember my name, although I doubt it would do you all any good after I am done with you poor darlings, tsk tsk tsk!'

With a manic fervour wrapped in a malicious intention, Madam Petunia Yates broke into the little-known song by Azalea Williams—a renowned protégé of Dahlia Brown—changing her lyrics here and there to suit her whims while alarming everyone present with her untimely appearance.

Dark petunia under the moon
Grows wild into the night
Climbing the branches of my soul
Tonight
You all will die
Follow me deep into the abyss
And I, I know why
The stars will cry and die

Into the tomb of the night
And I, I know why
You'll never see the light
Now, follow the sin in the devil's eyes
Come straight into hell
Dark petunia under the moon
Dancing in the night sky
You can see them shining in my eyes
Midnight
Is here quite soon
Moonlight bends the sway of time
And I, I wish you death
Screaming in pain
At the sole of my shoes
And I, I wish you pain
At losing your one soul
Now, follow the sin in the devil's eyes
Come straight into hell

'If you are here to stop Chang Hong Lian from erasing the evidence, you might as well don't bother,' Inspector Abdul Rahman said to Madam Petunia Yates, trying to calm the tension in the room and avoid a battle between the ghosts that would surely end the lives of the living presently in the annexe building. 'She won't be going ahead with it because she just realized she was under a spell,' the inspector tried to explain on Hong Lian's behalf to save his own skin as well as that of Ernest's.

Deep in his heart, the Inspector already knew it wasn't as simple as what Madam Petunia Yates had made it out to be— instincts had told him that she was here to do more than just killing a ghost. Which murderer announced their names before doing the deed? Was she not afraid that he could link her name to that of another? Marguerite Daisy Holmes for example? Her own daughter? Did she mean to silence him and Ernest, too, forever?

'That's a pity,' Madam Petunia remarked nonchalantly as she checked the condition of her well-manicured nails. It would be good if she could end Hong Lian using a good excuse as a cover, but she could also drop all pretences and cut to the chase. She was here primarily to cut lives after all. 'Stop trying to save your pitiful life. You are pathetic.'

'No, you are the pathetic one,' Hong Lian retorted, coming to the inspector's defence as she placed the Broth of Oblivion onto a nearby table next to Ernest who looked uncomfortable at the impending confrontation. Did this ghost need reminding that she, Hong Lian, had bested her before in Marguerite Daisy's luxurious home? *It seems that some lessons do bear repeating,* she thought and itched for a fight, just for the heck of it because some people, or in this case, a ghost, needed to relearn some things.

She did initially come here to fight, didn't she? This might just as well be, although she must admit that she hadn't really expected to fight on the side of the Inspector and Ernest, to be frank. The universe was indeed full of twists and turns, she observed, and before the night was out, there would surely be more of those coming her way.

'Me, pathetic?' Madam Petunia Yates laughed aloud at Hong Lian's insolence, knowing she would have to teach this petulant Chinese ghost a bloody lesson that she would never forget.

Letting Hong Lian win the other time was a matter of strategic importance. She herself and her beloved daughter, Marguerite Daisy, needed a borrowed knife to do their dirty work—kill Chang Pai Lian and Adrian Holmes on a rampage, which the deranged Red Lotus Ghost had failed to do! Now, it got in that girl's big head that she was better than her, an insult that needed to be repaid in blood many times over, of course.

'Enough with the chit-chat, you really want to do this or not?' Madam Petunia Yates asked, her voice tinged with a note of impatience as she gripped her enchanted brolly tightly, 'I haven't got all night, you know.'

'By all means, let's dance with the Grim Reaper if you so insist,' Hong Lian taunted Madam Petunia Yates as she swirled her sleeves to reveal her twin blades hidden underneath them. In several deft martial art moves, she backflipped and somersaulted while clashing her twin blades together in a display of power and grace.

She came prepared—out of the shadows came the funeral paper effigies playing *jinghu* and *erhu* fiddles, *yuequin* mandolin, as well as *pipa* and *xianzi* lutes to the tune of *The Ballad of Mulan*. An army of warrior paper effigies branding various weapons of war like spears, axes, swords, maces, rope-darts, and arrows from the play came forward. The ballad had some three hundred lines to be sung and memorized but the battle would be over way before the play did, she reckoned. 'Yield now or it is over for you,' Hong Lian threatened Madam Petunia Yates.

'Ah . . . it's a dance-off! It ain't over till the fat lady sings,' Madam Petunia Yates quipped in jest as she opened her enchanted brolly and swirled it, bringing to life Italian opera in all its grandeur, perfect with its allegro, adagio, as well as crescendo.

To everyone's utter surprise, Madam Petunia Yates had just re-enacted *The Story of Tosca* by way of her dark magic—an opera masterpiece that chronicled the fall of the Roman Republic in the Battle of Marengo, its characters played by the souls of the dead from the actual battle of centuries past.

'Don't take it the wrong way, my dear, but I prefer Italian opera,' Madam Petunia Yates declared, eager to pit her skills against Hong Lian's. She had expected the other twin, Pai Lian, to come here, but to her surprise it was Hong Lian instead—having come back from hell. No thanks to the interference from the other sister! Whether it was the White or Red Lotus ghost, it mattered not as both would eventually go back to hell again where they belonged, one way or another, when she had her terrible ways with them, she swore.

'Death by opera, I don't know if I should cry or laugh,' Ernest remarked with much apathy, himself very much a fan of modern music as he held on to his coconut while the Inspector held the other one. He didn't have the time to go with their plan to plant the coconuts in bins and was feeling rather silly and out of place watching the fierce battle unfolding before his eyes. In frustration, Ernest prompted the Inspector sarcastically, 'Anytime now. Tell me when we should break into that "Cocomo" song.'

A battle was fought, both inside and outside the Annex building, with mercy neither asked for nor given—a general paper effigy on horseback with a Qinglong spear mounted with crescent blade sliced off the head of Barone Scarpia's soul, Rome's chief of police. The soul of the political prisoner Cesare Angelotti fired a shot at a commander paper effigy with a battle-axe, felling him onto the ground, bloodied and raw. The souls of the firing squad at Castel Sant'Angelo fired shots at the royal archers, both sides sustaining heavy losses.

As fury and bloodshed intensified, music and fire roared with a vengeance in tune with the rising bloodlust. On the other side of the building, Hong Lian slashed with her twin swords at Madam Petunia Yates who parried her attacks with her enchanted brolly as a shield—the former landing a lucky cut across the latter's face.

Ahh . . . the deepest cut would bring about the darkest scar, Hong Lian thought, but this pain was more of an insult that would result in the worst retaliation from Madam Petunia Yates.

To Hong Lian's surprise, she saw the old witch wasn't what she appeared to be, as the outflowing bad blood revealed squirming vermins, gnats, maggots, and worms underneath her well-preserved complexion—the latter was as different on the inside as she was on the outside, like night and day. Even more shocking was that Madam Petunia Yates remained unfazed as she casually dabbed a finger on her wound and lapped up the blood while smiling menacingly.

'I'll teach you why it is unwise to bring a knife to a gun fight, my dear,' Madam Petunia Yates said to Hong Lian as she opened her enchanted brolly and flew to the dark sky amidst the shrieking of banshees and dead souls screaming.

By twirling her brolly, cyclones started swirling, ripping everything in sight before a bolt of lightning hit Hong Lian in her heart, knocking her out cold—a shock so terrible that both Ernest and Inspector Abdul Rahman accidentally dropped their coconuts which detonated with an eldritch force that swept across the spiritual sphere, knocking Madam Petunia Yates off from the sky.

What fell from the night sky was anything but a human soul, scurrying hurriedly about like a charred demonic entity on all fours before gathering its instincts to feed on Hong Lian's soul.

'I'll suck the sins out of you,' it yelped in agony and distress as it hopped onto Hong Lian and hungrily began sucking the essences of the latter's immortal soul only to be suddenly splashed with the Broth of Oblivion by Ernest and accidentally ingesting the 'soul-ution' with devastating effects.

'What? Where? Who?' the bewildered entity that was once Madam Petunia Yates hollered in confusion having lost all its memories and sense of self due to the magical ingredients of the broth. Even Madam Petunia's much-vaunted killer instincts were all gone, along with her abilities to wield the arcane arts.

But the effects of the spiritual detonation had alarming repercussions, sending ripples across realities right down to hell alerting the Heibai Wuchang guardians from the netherworld— the powerful black and white deities of impermanence tasked to escort spirits of the dead to be judged in hell. So formidable they were that they could permanently erase even the souls of the lesser gods with but a single thought!

Beware beware . . . black and white shadows
are rising,
The blazing coals are sparkled, hellfire is raging.
Come, come . . . die by night's end with much sorrow,
Your sins will be paid like there is no tomorrow.

Like a fire storm from the deepest pits of hell, both Heibai Wuchang guardians rose from the netherworld and roared with fury, releasing their long, long tongues of red as their black and white shadows traversed the land and warped the reality around them, ripping and dragging the lost souls of the paper effigies and the fallen dead from the Battle of Marengo into the dark abyss.

In one fell swoop, both black and white deities smashed the dark entity that was once Madam Petunia Yates with their spiked clubs, dragging and dumping her corpse back into a hellhole. And then, the duo moved on to Chang Hong Lian and raised their spiked clubs together.

'Stop, I beg of you,' Ernest yelled and cried, having found his courage to save the soul of a pitiful ghost. With sincere prayers echoing in his heart and tears of grace raining on his cheeks, he interceded on behalf of the Red Lotus ghost who had no one by her side.

He knew Pai Lian would have given up her immortal soul for her twin sister, but she was not here—he was. The least he could do was to repay the kindness of his benefactor for saving him from suicide the other time and for ghostwriting his book. In his heart, kindness should beget kindness—he knew Pai Lian would have wanted him to.

'I want to save Hong Lian from suffering in hell,' Ernest declared and fell on his knees before the Heibai Wuchang guardians, while racking his wits to think of a plan. Then, he recalled how Pai Lian did it and he decided to take a page from her book, well technically his book. He needed to trade her soul with something they wanted, but what would it be?

'I want to trade Hong Lian's soul with this enchanted brolly,' Ernest said aloud as he grabbed it from the ground—it was coincidentally lying next to him by providence and by luck, oh how the universe worked in mysterious ways. He was always fortunate that way. *Well, its mistress is dead, already bound for the deepest level of hell*, he thought, *and that's made me the new master; finders, keepers!*

'Ahh . . . the long-lost enchanted brolly from hell, crafted with the bone of a boar demon, a worthy weapon indeed,' the Black Wuchang guardian said in a sonorous voice, nodding his head in approval. With a sigh, he explained to Ernest about kindness, 'It's beyond your knowledge right now, but learn to let go . . . her soul is better off renewed, don't let her dwell in her current misery or more mistakes will follow.'

'But make no mistake, we will still accept your trade,' the White Wuchang guardian told Ernest, noting that the entity that was once Madam Petunia Yates had sucked the sins off Hong Lian already and had unwittingly died for her. A compromise was in order, he thought. 'Your friend can bypass the suffering of hell. We will place her on the Naihe bridge to be reborn. Do you accept our terms?'

'I accept,' Ernest declared, having decided not to push his luck. Hong Lian was living on borrowed time anyway and her forty-nine days would soon be up; best to take advantage of the offer before the guardians changed their minds. It was rather amusing, he thought, that the universe had a sense of humour. The girl who was murdered and dumped under the Taiping bridge now got to walk the Naihe Bridge unscathed from suffering, a 180-degree turn that was.

'I accept,' Ernest reiterated his consent, fearing the Heibai Wuchang guardians would revoke their offer. What remained now was to explain everything to the other twin, Chang Pai Lian, a prospect that Ernest found to be quite challenging. No one wanted to be the bearer of bad news, even if it was in some ways good.

25

Has he been left alone to cope with this shame?
It was all over the papers, she gave out his name.
He's a two-timer, a criminal, give him the rope!
He's unrepentant, for him there's no hope!

The morning papers had brought more bad news for Adrian Holmes, once a renowned bestselling author of crime novels, now denigrated to the pariah of society with the exposés his wife, Marguerite Daisy, had been feeding the press and the tabloids. She didn't just come with baseless accusations but was armed with scandalous proofs of photos, videos, motel chits, restaurant receipts, and the likes, enough evidence to fell even the pillars of society.

How she got hold of the evidences was questionable, but one thing was certain—she wanted him dead in the eyes of society. Hell hath no fury like a woman scorned, he would probably end up dead for real by day's end if she had her way . . . as dead as Jasmine Somasundram, the lawyer he had commissioned to draft out the divorce papers, her death splashed ignominiously across the main page on account that the attack had taken place at a police station.

He had hoped for help from the dead, but the ghost of his lover, Chang Pai Lian, was nowhere to be found. She had not visited him in days despite promising to exonerate him by taking all the blame. He couldn't count on his dim-witted half-brother,

Anthony Holmes either—God bless his poor soul—whom he had used to get rid of his pregnant lover, Chang Hong Lian. That poor, poor fool could only haunt his dreams with gibberish warnings about The Hanged Man.

What was that all about anyway? Why the hangman's noose? Was the spirit of his stupid half-brother, Anthony, still looking out for his best interest despite what he had done to the poor man? Did the fool really think sharing the same father automatically made them loyal brothers? Why so naïve, this man? Or was Anthony being a jerk from beyond? Taunting him with hangman's noose knowing he was on trial for murder? That would only happen if the Malaysian government found him guilty of murder. A big 'if', that was. Had it not cross Anthony's dim-witted mind that he would be freed once Pai Lian took the blame? Hah, he would like to see Anthony's face then!

'Lunch time!' the guard yelled as he knocked his baton repeatedly on Adrian's prison bars with a loud din. Looking at the prisoner dismissively as though proven guilty already, he barked at Adrian rudely, 'After lunch, you've got fifteen minutes to exercise at the open courtyard!'

Adrian chose not to retort and anger the guard although he was seething inside at being treated in this manner. Oh well, this was a prison, not exactly the Ritz. That guard could do worse with his baton, especially at night with no security cameras around in the communal showers. Woe would be his ass when he accidentally dropped his soap.

He took his tray and saw lunch was just a bowl of fish ball soup prepared with yellow *mee*. A few anchovies floated dismally around a leaf of lettuce with fish balls swimming lethargically in onion soup. Tears nearly burst from his eyes but he held them back lest the other prisoners think he was weak. In this place, being weak was a death sentence.

'No, no, no,' he muttered when he saw the newspaper lining his tray and almost dropped his lunch—the guard had purposely put an article featuring Marguerite Daisy playing victim in front of the press and accusing Adrian of multiple marital affairs. He almost choked with indignation even though it was true—she had strategically moved her chess piece faster than he could before his divorce papers could be drawn out. His loss!

When he was out of prison, revenge would be his. He could always fight back and she would be the one pushing daisies from six feet underground. Ahh . . . the things he would do once he escaped the prison bars—a feast at Bobino Milano Restaurant & Bar in Italy came to mind. They had the best spaghetti, not this yellow mee!

He could feel a tear running down his face as he sat in his cell, the loneliest place he knew. All he could think of was his lover, Pai Lian, and he needed her to be here. He wiped away his falling tear and hit the floor on bended knees, 'Please, please come save me!'

Then, looking at his meagre meal, he realized there was something strange; a string of yellow *mee* had floated to the top and become entangled like a hangman's noose! Was this a joke? Was it the guard's doing? Was it Anthony's spirit? Was it God? Who did this, he wondered as fear gripped his beating heart. Was this a premonition for things to come? Was it certain that he would die by the hangman's noose?

He scuttled to his prison corner and cowered there in the dark, trembling with much fear and weeping inconsolably. Was his time on earth up? Was this how he would die? The Malaysian government convicting him and sending him to the hangman's gallows? No, he didn't want to die, not yet! He had many things to live for! He was rich, damn it! He wanted to enjoy his wealth and all!

'Stop your dramatics, this is not *Sandiwara Minggu Ini*!' the guard warned Adrian when he saw the latter trembling in a dark corner like a rat—a little over the top, not unlike the weekly dramedy show on telly—while he was making his rounds in the cell block.

'If you're not having lunch, go for your fifteen-minute exercise at the open courtyard,' the guard told Adrian, seeing that it was about to rain. These breaks didn't come often—only once a week—and he would hate to see any prisoner missing out on the opportunity. That much of concession he would give any prisoner, even though in his mind Adrian was already guilty as the proverbial butler.

Upon hearing what the guard had said, Adrian got up with much effort, eager for a breather and a timeout. He wiped away his falling tears as the guard unlocked his prison cell and ushered him out to the hallway that led to the open courtyard.

As he walked along the hallway, his eyes darted cautiously to the dark shadowy corners fearing his death was lying in wait. His emotions weighed heavily in his chest like the bodies of the deceased he had put to rest. He felt stifled by gripping terror, the kind that made his lungs hurt and palms sweat. It almost felt like the hallway walls were closing in on him, trying to knock him into his coffin, but he dismissed it as a hallucination of his fear.

Nervously he braved the lonely pathway and shot furtive glances at the dark corners along the hallway where the cobwebs hung—their intricate lines of light had turned grey from dust over the years. Then, spiders came crawling out in droves on the ceiling, spinning cobwebs not of their usual wheels with concentrical circles but of hangman's nooses drooping all over the ceiling that sent chills down his spine. Incredibly, the guard made no note of this and was totally oblivious to the surroundings. It could all be in his head, Adrian thought; it must all be due to stress, he hoped.

Next, they reached the gatekeepers at an intersection checkpoint and a lady officer with a long pigtail braid broke away from the group to unlock the gate for them. As she turned away and sauntered back to her desk, Adrian noticed her long pigtail braid was in the shape of a hangman's noose. This couldn't be a coincidence, not at all. Was the universe trying to tell him something? Or was something more sinister happening?

'This is it, enjoy yourself,' the guard escorting Adrian said. He pushed open the heavy metal door to reveal the open landscaped courtyard with big trees and long flowering vines—a view to die for—exactly what the other condemned prisoners had often wistfully remarked because they were denied access to the outside world. But to Adrian Holmes, it portended death and destruction because he was the only one who could see the long flowering vines turning into hangman's nooses.

'Take me back to my cell please,' a teary-eyed Adrian begged the guard who was escorting him, knowing his end would come soon. Most would want to die outside in the sunshine and amongst the trees, but as remorse would dictate, he didn't feel he deserved such a death. He knew his death would be a violent, bloody, and painful affair. He would be better off to take his own life with his own belt than be a victim to what would be coming for him.

In any case, it would be difficult to take his own life out here in the open courtyard with the guards lurking at every corner. It would definitely end up a futile attempt and worse still, it would be a spectacle for all to see. No, it would be more discreet to die on his own terms in the privacy of his own cell. There was not much time, he was on the clock, *tick-tock, tick-tock*. He had to do it quickly or he would die a very bad death, he feared.

'O . . . Okay,' the guard replied unsurely, wondering who in the right mind would want to forfeit his hard-earned break for the week. Was Adrian now a suicide risk, he began to wonder? Should he alert the authorities? 'Let's go back to your cell then.'

'Give me your belt before you go in,' the guard demanded of Adrian. He might not be privy to the supernatural disturbances, but he knew a suicide risk when he saw one. This prisoner was a nervous wreck, spooked beyond his sanity, but he did surrender his belt without any protest. 'Now, you can go inside while I lock your gate,' the guard told Adrian and made a mental note to alert his superiors of potential dangers and put the prisoner under suicide watch.

Adrian dashed into his cell like there was no tomorrow, he was losing too much time he didn't have. Either he committed suicide now on his own terms or he would die a violent death at the hands of whatever horror that was coming his way. With his belt gone, he had to find something else quickly. No to the toothbrush, yes to the shaver's razor blade . . . but he was unfortunately too late.

> No more time to enjoy his wealth,
> No more time to indulge in pleasures,
> No more time for chasing dreams,
> No more rainbows to take delight in.

Now, there was no more time to do anything as reality in Adrian's cell warped into a hellish one with a terrifying entity emerging before him in full view—screeching with so much anger that he couldn't turn a deaf ear to it, and carrying a vicious hangman's noose that he couldn't turn a blind eye to.

Enter The Hanged Man, the twelfth entity from the major arcana tarot deck, who was the living embodiment of sacrifice, delusion, surrender, and persecution. Invariably, this one was about letting go of lives. In less time than it took for a fall to break a bone, The Hanged Man swung his noose and caught Adrian Holmes by the neck with its loop before hollering aloud:

> Noose drawn from the depth of sin,
> Hold your head and hang down low.
> Scream in horror and make a din,
> Suffer in pain and death will follow.

Adrian screamed and shouted for the guards, letting it all out from the bottom of his lungs. He freaked out and struggled in terror but no one could hear his distress, not in a warped hell. Before he knew it, he was swinging across his cell, knocking off tables and chairs as well as smashing glasses and mugs into smithereens.

'Please, please let me go,' he cried out in despair and begged for mercy that he knew he wouldn't get. In fact, it got worse for him as the noose was magically transformed into a barbed wire and ripped the flesh of his neck to the bone. It didn't stop there. As though that was not enough torture, The Hanged Man turned his noose into a burning chain link and seared Adrian's open wounds with it while laughing cruelly like the sadistic monster that he was.

'I . . . I know who sent you,' Adrian managed to say despite the immense pain and the trauma inflicted unto him, not that it would matter much, seeing that he was already on his way to hell. 'Never expected her to be this . . . this v . . . vicious,' he remarked regretfully to no one in particular at his epiphany.

For the coup de grâce, The Hanged Man transformed his noose into a long belt and hoisted Adrian up to the ceiling fan, stringing him up like a piece of carcass at a butcher shop. As the warped reality in the cell dissipated like a trick of the light and reverted to what was before, the belt magically re-transformed into the belt that Adrian had earlier, right down to its brand and colour . . . the very same one that the guard had confiscated earlier, which left everyone at the force bewildered, including the forensic team that was assigned to make sense of the whole incident.

By all accounts, the security video revealed nothing, just images of Adrian preparing to do the deed with his belt . . . the one that he didn't have. More baffling still was an unexplained tarot card, The Hanged man, present in the cell— a calling card from hell to taunt the authorities for years to come.

I know the names of all the flowers,
And I know that red lotus in the pond.
My tears fall quickly as I quietly cower,
Just hearing her name, losing our bond.

Across the bridge to a new life, she goes,
Only in dreams I get to see her face.
But my nights are sleepless, full of woes,
If only I could die instead, in her place.

There was nothing more that I, Chang Pai Lian, could say, knowing my twin, Chang Hong Lian, was gone from my life forever; across the Naihe Bridge to her new life, leaving me alone to mourn our memories. She won't even know my face, nor would she remember our lives and deaths together—the Broth of Oblivion was to blame.

I wasn't the only one stricken by loss, Marguerite Daisy Holmes, too, was suffering. Her sadness flowed freely with her mother, Madam Petunia Yates', departure; wave after wave of tears flooded her senses, drowning her in sorrow and madness. Not even the return of her precious South Sea pearl necklace could alleviate her pain. It had reappeared mysteriously one day at her luxurious Kamunting residence via Grab delivery of all things.

Revenge was addictive,
it drove Marguerite Daisy insane,
destroyed her inner peace,
and swapped it with bitter madness.

Revenge was sweet,
it was best served cold like a dessert,
ice-cold like her soul,
and a fire borne from her darkness.

Poor, poor Adrian Holmes, he didn't even wait for the Malaysian government to hang him—he ended himself with his own belt in his own cell, as the press would want the world to believe.

Wicked, wicked Marguerite Daisy Holmes, she didn't even wait for the law to run its course—she ended him in his own cell by way of magic with Lady Nightshade's help, I believe.

Who else would leave The Hanged Man tarot card as a calling card? They obviously wanted me to know. Had I not been away in hell saving my twin sister, I would be there to defend him, I swore to all in heaven, earth, and hell.

Often I wonder what my life would be like,
If I didn't have Adrian Holmes in my life.
I died and had come back only to see,
That I wouldn't be a ghost without him or me.

I wanted to spend my life loving him though,
Even when I suffered the hell he put me through.
I was so sorry, and I said it with all my heart,
He didn't love me and now death made us part.

Goodbye, Adrian Holmes, our heartache was at its end but we already knew in consolation that we couldn't fix what had already been broken. My heart was in a million pieces, your life was full of hits and misses. We should have known our affair couldn't last if the only place we were searching for love was in our past. We had no future and our deaths proved it all.

It's the last chapter of my story,
I dedicate it to the man I've saved.
It was friendship in all its glory,
You are the friend that I crave.

Yes, I am ashamed of my past,
But I am the happiest ghost alive.
A love like mine wouldn't last,
Still, I want you to live your best life.

I'll rewrite your fate with a book,
Set you high to fame and fortune.
High above the stars you'll look,
Your destiny is one most fortunate.

It's the last chapter of my story,
I wish I'd known you in my living years.
Be happy always, never be sorry,
I'll say my goodbye, so no more tears.

26

As she typed 'The End' with a heavy heart, the White Lotus ghost knew hers wasn't too far away—she had to face Lady Nightshade in a showdown tonight at Marguerite Daisy's luxurious holiday bungalow in Kamunting, Taiping. As hard as she tried, she did not forget the fact that she was already damned for eternity for stealing the Key to Hell crystal pendant too.

Time would come, time would go—there would come a time when one wouldn't know which way to go, and right now, she was at that crossroad. She didn't even know if there would be any redemption for her at all. Everything was so overwhelming; she would cry endless tears although she had promised herself not to. Admittedly, she had never felt so alone until now, so abandoned in her despair.

But she mustn't give in to her despair, not now, she knew she would not relent, like the lofty lotuses in Taiping Botanical Garden, swaying in the storm and night tempest, and rising again with the dawn . . . She would rise too, the White Lotus Ghost vowed, unbroken, unshaken, and rising from her dire pain.

It was not like she didn't have any weapon to defend herself—granted she no longer had the Key to Hell crystal pendant having surrendered it to Ox Head already, but she still had that venomous fang from the elephant-swallowing BaShe serpent from hell. This huge fang was a veritable curved sabre in her hands, deadly in its poison that could kill hellish beasts and lesser gods. It had mysteriously disappeared mid-fight while she was wielding the

Key to Hell crystal pendant's teleportation powers, and then
reappeared under Ernest's bed in the human realm, a most
fortuitous turn of event for her. Thank you, God!

It might not be the *fúchén* horsetail flywhisk called Cloud-
Killer from Horse Face or the *Niu Wang* bullwhip from Ox Head
that she had initially planned to procure from hell, but it was what
providence had provided her and she was thankful for it. At least
she had a dangerous weapon to show for the showdown with
Lady Nightshade and Marguerite Daisy.

Never underestimate the rage of a woman or a ghost with
nothing to lose—she literally went through hell and back, what
pain or suffering didn't she know of? She didn't underestimate
Lady Nightshade either—someone who once had the Key to Hell
crystal pendant would be an adversary to watch out for.

An unimaginably powerful magical artefact favoured by
the ten Yama Kings of Hell in the hands of an insignificant
psychic medium? Something was not right; didn't anyone
notice it before? They could fool the whole world, but not this
ex–crime ghostwriter. Lady Nightshade was the hidden dragon
to Madam Petunia Yates' crouching tiger—the former was a
secretive adversary hiding in plain sight while the latter was
more of an overt enemy out in the open, she'd reckon. Before
the night was out, the White Lotus ghost was sure she would
be inundated with more surprises.

As if a harbinger of things to come, a bolt of lightning
slashed past the heavy rain clouds as thunder roared and
reverberated the silent earth, revealing the White Lotus Ghost's
location—she had written the last pages of her manuscript only
hours earlier and here she was in the back forest of Marguerite
Daisy's luxurious holiday bungalow in Taiping where she was
doing a covert stake-out amidst the coconut trees.

The wind picked up speed and the scent of rain gave way to
pummelling showers. In a blink of an eye, the sky turned black
with rage, as dark as Lady Nightshade's sombre mood.

'How the hell did you sneak in here without us knowing?' the annoyed psychic medium asked to which the White Lotus ghost only shrugged. There was really no point in giving up her secrets just yet, she decided; not when she spotted Marguerite Daisy sitting quietly on her vast porch, trying to be inconspicuous with her South Sea pearl necklace around her neck—*that has got to be a secret weapon*, the White Lotus ghost surmised, *no doubt to be used against me.*

'You are the psychic, you tell me,' the Whit Lotus ghost taunted Lady Nightshade sarcastically, still watching Marguerite Daisy closely from the corner of her eyes. With a sad sigh, she braced her aching heart to hear what they had to say about murdering Adrian Holmes, 'Did you have to kill him? You could have wiped away his memories with your spells, you know?'

'That man-whore deserved it, worse than a piece of *man-ure*,' Lady Nightshade replied and laughed wickedly before retaliating with a nasty repartee, 'If you miss him, you can join him six feet under, pushing daisies.'

'I'll leave that to you, you piece of murderous filth,' the White Lotus Ghost shot back, aware that she was here to bury her enemies. She didn't have all night and the clock was ticking away furiously; she had to use her time on earth judiciously.

'Tonight, you'll dine in hell with Lady Petunia Yates,' she told them, having just about enough she could stomach from the likes of them, 'Or do you prefer a high tea invitation instead?'

'Have a care when you speak my protégée's name,' Lady Nightshade warned the White Lotus Ghost, hissing with rage as Marguerite Daisy squirmed in her seat by the porch, visibly distressed at the mention of her mother. 'Never ever speak her name in vain!' she thundered in anger.

So, the White Lotus Ghost was right after all, the great and powerful Madam Petunia Yates was just a protégée to Lady Nightshade. It did make sense, no? The witch from beyond was only contactable via psychic mediums and could only travel via accursed objects damned by the latter. In both instances, they had to rely on psychic mediums . . . like Lady Nightshade.

But how did Madam Petunia Yates get so powerful? She didn't sell her soul to the devil, did she?

'I did not teach my protégée the arcane arts in life and in death for her to die like that,' Lady Nightshade screamed in infuriation, her eyes watering at the massive loss of her favourite spirit. In exasperation, she ripped off her sleeve to reveal a long scar on her upper left arm and snarled, 'I did not lose a bone to craft her a weapon to fail like this.'

Her bone was the power behind that enchanted brolly? That woman really had a bad bone in her.

'But the time for talk has passed, now is the hour for your death,' Lady Nightshade shrieked and took out her deck of major arcana tarot cards—a stunning 1425 Visconti-Sforza set by the looks of it, hand-painted with oil paint, gold and silver.

'Meet your doom, enter *The Hanged Man*!' she said, and threw down a card that warped reality with its brilliant flash of light, releasing the living embodiment of the tarot piece—a terrifying hanged man with a magical rope, marching and singing, going all out for the kill.

> Noose drawn from the depth of sin,
> Hold your head and hang down low.
> Scream in horror and make a din,
> Suffer in pain and death will follow.

In less time than it took for the White Lotus ghost to scream, The Hanged Man threw his magical rope at her and had its noose looped around her neck, squeezing the soul out of the White Lotus ghost as she screamed in pain.

To torment her further, he magically transformed his rope into a vine of thorns and trashed the White Lotus ghost around on the dirt ground to make her bleed from the bites of its vicious spikes.

'Your lover died by a rope of belts,' The Hanged Man revealed to her, his menacing eyes relishing in the memory of Adrian Holmes' pain while transforming his magical rope into a long metal cable he used to electrocute the White Lotus ghost. 'But that would be too merciful for you!'

'Argh . . .' she screamed in horror and pain as jolts of electricity coursed through her, shocking her senselessly as she reacted the only way she could—cutting the cable in one swift motion with her BaShe fang sabre that was concealed underneath her sleeves.

To everyone's shock, that stopped The Hanged Man in his tracks—the White Lotus ghost's retaliation with her weapon sent an unexpected chain reaction that resulted in her adversary breaking into blisters with venom foaming out of his mouth. It also delivered eternal death as the tarot card burnt into ashes and sparkles of ember floated away in the night air, much to Lady Nightshade's chagrin and Marguerite Daisy's dismay.

'T . . . That cannot be!' Lady Nightshade stammered in disbelief. Never once in her long years had something like this happened. Then again, she had not met someone as tenacious as the White Lotus ghost was—one who had stolen her Key to Hell crystal pendant and now destroyed her Hanged Man tarot card.

'You will pay for this, you nasty ghost, I swear you will!' Lady Nightshade snapped in fury and took out another tarot piece from her major arcana deck. With a smirk and a huff, she glanced at the card before breaking a smile. 'Let's see how you deal with The Magician and his dark magic, shall we?' she teased the White Lotus ghost, knowing very well the latter wouldn't like it one bit.

Reality came crashing down as soon as the tarot card hit the ground, bringing about a massive whirlwind in the clouds that spat lightning onto the ground. Out of the fissure on earth's crust, an imposing figure rose from the ruin—The Magician had made his grand entrance!

My magic is like the dramatic drift,
Of evil straight from the devil's roar.

    And smoke and mirrors from the rift,
    Of celebrating death as corpses soar.

Out of his tall hat, The Magician released the doves of despair that cursed all present with a lethal mix of hopelessness and desolation as misery and anguish consumed their bodies and souls. Out came the White Lotus ghost's secret weapon, Bomoh Mona Mawar; like a raving lunatic affected by the dove's devastation. Out of the blue, Ernest Maxwell Graves also appeared unexpectedly—even when the White Lotus ghost had asked him not to come here—keeling over in so much anguish due to the onslaught by The Magician.

'Ahh . . . I see you didn't come alone,' Lady Nightshade commented, her lips pursed in anger while her mind found the reason as to why they hadn't discovered the White Lotus ghost's presence earlier. To be able to cloak from her clairvoyance and foresight could only mean one thing—she had help from a powerful witch doctor, in this case, Bomoh Mona Mawar.

'It is all an exercise in futility,' she remarked in a matter-of-fact tone, after summing up the odds in her mind. She still had aces up her sleeves, and she doubted they could surmount her challenges even if the motley crew worked together. 'You are all done for anyway. You don't even know what you are up against, my dears.'

'Neither do you,' Bomoh Mona Mawar yelled as she unleashed a barrage of *jarum susuk* golden needles from her soul at The Magician—directly hitting him in his eyes, on his face and body, driving him to a berserker rage.

She stood there, visibly shaken after the release of her golden needles, evidently aged beyond her years. *Never mind*, she thought to herself, *I could always add more needles later to look younger, maybe this time, eighteen years old.*

'You *henti sekarang* or I will show you no mercy, *tau*!' Bomoh Mona Mawar yelled aloud at Lady Nightshade and Marguerite Daisy to stop as she stood astride in defiance, her words left no doubt as to her intention if she and her friends were threatened further.

'Pain, terrible pain,' The Magician screamed in agony as Bomoh Mona Mawar's witchcraft inflicted unimaginable damage to body and soul. As a parting shot, he took out his magic wand to cast a spell of fire, '*Ignis ignis lucidus, incende omnes!*'

In a quick move that belied her age, the witch doctor beat him to it with a reverse spell, '*Kilab gnupmak manat gnugaj*,' which rerouted the ball of fire right back at The Magician, ending him in cinders as his magic wand dropped onto the ground with a clang and rolled towards Ernest.

'Y . . . You didn't just say "*Balik kampung tanam jagung*", did you?' a bewildered Ernest complained with a look of incredulity on his face, disbelieving his ears when he heard the witch taunted her nemesis to go back to the village and plant . . . corn. So unbelievable that something so childish could be an actual spell!

Without meaning to, Ernest coughed up wisps of cinder from his mouth as he picked up the magic wand in front of him. *Never look a gift horse in the mouth*, he decided, *not after the enchanted brolly incident*. 'It sure sounded like the spell was spelt backwards that way,' he groaned in utter embarrassment for Bomoh Mona Mawar.

'What do you know about magic?' she retorted, eyes rolling in mock exasperation. She was an accomplished witch doctor, hailing from a long line of shamans from their days in Aceh, Sumatra. So, what if her methods were a little bizarre, some would say ridiculous? They worked, didn't they? '*Eh, you mesti believe tau? Believe kuat-kuat it'll work, tau?*' she tried teaching Ernest a thing or two about handling magic, flailing her hands about and crunching her fingers into a fist in conviction to demonstrate her point.

'Like this?' Ernest asked as he flicked the magic wand unsurely, causing it to erupt with a shower of colourful glitter of gold and silver that came out of nowhere from a unicorn's ass onto Lady Nightshade and Marguerite Daisy, adding unintentional insult to their defeat in their hands. 'Oops, sorry . . .' he only managed to apologize sheepishly at his gaffe.

'You frigging bastards!' Lady Nightshade snapped in anger at their indignity as she spat out a mouthful of glitter from her mouth and rubbed her eyes. She glanced at Marguerite Daisy who struggled to brush away the glitter from her immaculate tresses and expensive Prada dress. 'Do you know how long it takes for these to come off?' Lady Nightshade yelled at them, before casting another tarot card at them, 'That's it, I curse death unto you!'

An explosion of dark light began where her words ended, haunting the night with promises of death as the stars in heaven retreated in fright and the moon veiled her light behind clouds in fear. A hooded skeletal figure appeared silently like a phantom of the night, bringing with him doom and gloom as he sang a funeral dirge.

> Dark skies are falling, death is calling.
> Your clothes soaked in red, cry now in dread.
> Die in the shadows, die in the gallows.
> Your end comes near, your screams I hear.

A fight till death ensued and the White Lotus ghost would mourn its outcome, she knew—if they must die, let it not be in vain. She could hear Death calling her name, 'Pai Lian, Pai Lian, come meet your doom,' but she refused the sweet surrender to nothingness and vowed to fight till her last breath.

A scythe came crushing down onto the White Lotus ghost and she rolled away in the nick of time, avoiding its vicious impact as it lacerated the earth instead. She swung her BaShe fang sabre at its wielder, hitting his leg bone with a lucky strike . . . expecting a chain reaction that would bring Death to his knees. Venomous blisters did form on his bones, but Death did not succumb—he was already dead anyway. *H . . . How to kill a living embodiment of death*, she wondered?

Seeing that the White Lotus ghost was in trouble, Bomoh Mona Mawar came to her aid by casting a spell of fire at Death, 'Rakab aid iapmas sugnah,' but to no avail. Death by cremation did not happen. Death had died and now he won't again.

She stood there transfixed by indecision, racking her brain and trying to find a solution; a distraction that cost her dearly— the White Lotus ghost saw Death's scythe finding its mark and slicing the witch doctor's body cruelly open, spilling her intestines in the most gruesome of ways, an end akin to *hara-kiri* that would take its time, causing even more suffering for the victim.

With tears streaming down her face knowing her end was near, the White Lotus ghost saw Bomoh Mona Mawar unleashing her *jarum susuk* golden needles at her killer in retaliation—this time, it did work on Death as he staggered about unsurely on his feet and roared in agony.

In a moment that made the White Lotus ghost proud, an epiphany dawned on Bomoh Mona Mawar as she breathed the word 'Life' aloud before looking at Ernest and mouthed the word, 'Believe.'

But of course, why didn't she think of it first, the White Lotus ghost wondered? Life was anathema to death, its antithesis in the universe. Bomoh Mona Mawar's *jarum susuk* golden needles sustained youth and vitality that worked against death in a manner of speaking!

Believe . . . the word must have echoed in Ernest's mind, and for a guy who had once attempted to commit suicide, he now had to channel all his belief in life—body and soul—into his magic wand, blasting it with the purest form of energy at Death, who perished out of this reality upon contact with an unearthly scream that could be heard in the pits of hell.

'Bagus . . .' the White Lotus ghost heard Bomoh Mona Mawar saying aloud with whatever breath she had left and gave Ernest a thumb's up. With her life energy ebbing away, she gave her thanks to the good universe, smiling at how it had worked in mysterious ways before casting her last spell with her last breath, '*Apalek hutaj!*'

In answer to her spell, all the coconuts in the back forest of Marguerite Daisy's luxurious holiday home started falling onto the ground, detonating with a series of powerful eldritch forces that spread like ripples of wildfires across the spiritual realm, knocking both Lady Nightshade and Marguerite Daisy off balance.

'Now, there is hell to pay,' Lady Nightshade warned as she got up groggily to find her footing, the back of her skin clearly torn with two scraggly wings projecting out. She casually flapped them, flexing her black feathers while helping Marguerite Daisy to rise on her feet.

It did not escape anyone's notice that Marguerite Daisy also had wings but hers were more of the leathery bat-like kind. She took a moment to flap her wings and adjusted her Prada dress before unclasping her South Sea pearl necklace and holding it in her right hand like a nun would hold a rosary. 'You want to tell them who we are before they die?' she asked Lady Nightshade as she placed her left hand on her hip, spoiling for a fight.

'W . . . Who are you?' Ernest asked, gobsmacked at the unholy sight. This was totally unexpected and could very well turn the tide in their favour since they didn't know what the hell was going on. What were they fighting? Who exactly were they up against? Both Ernest and the White Lotus ghost weren't sure, to be perfectly honest.

'You haven't made the connection yet? You are the one who stole my Key to Hell,' Lady Nightshade reminded the White Lotus ghost, still sore about losing what she had been entrusted to keep safe. 'You are the crime author, you tell me what's going on,' she urged the White Lotus ghost, smiling like a cat who had mice for dinner.

Ahh . . . *that* crystal pendant—in the hands of a lost soul like the White Lotus ghost, one could travel back and forth between earth and hell. In the hands of a deity, however, it could potentially take hell to earth or vice versa. It was a weapon of a dark god constructed solely to instigate Armageddon on earth, that much she knew. Wait a minute . . .

'Yes, I am a fallen angel or what you people call a demon,' she told the White Lotus ghost and Ernest. Whether branded as an angel or a demon, it all depended on who was writing the book, the victor would get to write history.

'One-third of angels were cast down to earth and I was one of them unfortunately, no thanks to the combined efforts of the other angels like Gerald, Kok Yu, and Wea Fung after I stole the Key to Hell crystal pendant from them,' she revealed. Then her face unexpectedly lighted up with pleasure reminiscing her time in Heavenly Eden, and her heart resolved to go back home again via the Heavenly Eden Tea House in Taiping. Not many people knew of the elevator in there that could take anyone to Heaven at the penthouse level or Hell at the basement level. Unfortunately, those three angels guarded the elevator and no one dared to try and challenge them, it would be a futile attempt to be sure.

'I am of the porcine kind, not the serpentine type, just so you know,' Lady Nightshade announced as though her enemies needed to know that.

'Well, what do you know? Pigs do fly,' Ernest quipped out of turn, his knack for saying the wrong thing at the wrong time acting up again. Fortunately, Lady Nightshade and Marguerite Daisy did not pay heed to him.

'Our darling here, Marguerite Daisy is a Nephilim, a hybrid of a fallen angel and a human host,' Lady Nightshade explained. She paused a little, knowing it was time to reveal a big secret. These folks would have a hard time wrapping their heads around this fact for sure, everyone did anyway.

'You've heard about her human mother, Madam Petunia Yates, my protégée of course,' she said and then proceeded to ask White Lotus ghost a question, 'But what do you know of her father?'

'One of the fallen angels, I would presume,' the White Lotus ghost replied succinctly since Lady Nightshade had said Marguerite Daisy was a Nephilim. That would mean Madam Petunia Yates had an amorous tryst with a fallen angel. Did she join a cult or something? Was that where she met her mentor, Lady Nightshade? 'But who? Hmm . . . don't tell me it was the Light-Bringer, the Morning Star?' the White Lotus ghost asked Lady Nightshade, although she had already suspected he was the one.

'Correct! You are smart,' Lady Nightshade complimented the White Lotus Ghost, confirming Marguerite Daisy was the daughter of the Red Dragon, like the latter needed proof that she was the devil's offspring.

'The Devil wears Prada,' Ernest quipped again at Marguerite Daisy's choice of high fashion brand, before self-correcting his earlier remark, 'The She-devil wears Prada.'

The White Lotus ghost wanted to laugh at Ernest sometimes, but that would only encourage him to make ridiculous out-of-turn remarks and embarrass her in public even more.

'Why not Balenciaga? Why Prada?' Ernest asked before the White Lotus ghost shushed him. There was more important information to fish for. Her taste in fashion was the last thing she needed to know but the precious South Sea pearl necklace was definitely right on top of her list. Their survival really depended on it, she was sure, even though she didn't quite know what it was just yet.

'What's with the pearl necklace?' the White Lotus ghost asked, cutting Ernest from asking his frivolous question. If it was anything like what she suspected it was, they were already doomed. 'A gift from daddy, I would guess. A weapon of mass destruction?'

'Oh, the Soul-keeper pearl necklace, you mean? It was a gift from mummy,' Marguerite Daisy replied, cutting Lady Nightshade before the latter could answer on her behalf as she strutted to the front of her porch. 'The world knows it as a precious piece of jewellery, worth $50 million, procured from the Celebes Sea, but it is actually priceless. Each lustrous pearl hosts the soul of an ancient dead god before mankind left the sea for land.'

'How did Madam Petunia Yates get it?' the White Lotus ghost had to ask Marguerite Daisy, hoping that her late mother didn't steal or kill for it. *Before mankind left the sea for land?* That jewellery was truly ancient and it came from another age . . . way before the dinosaur age. 'What does it do besides looking pretty?'

'My grandmother, Countess Wisteria Yates, was also a witch and with her powers she saw what those gold-lipped Pinctada oysters were hosting,' Marguerite Daisy explained. 'She hired divers to harvest the ancient pearls from the coral graveyard of the old gods and had them strung together. She bequeathed the pearl necklace to my mother, Lady Petunia Yates, on her wedding day.'

'I think these people are more interested to know what it does, my dear,' Lady Nightshade cajoled Marguerite Daisy into revealing its powers, gleefully eager for the latter to put the demon in demonstration for their enemies' so-called benefit.

Demon? She caught herself using that word. Well, these days even the old gods were demonized by people when their pantheon didn't fit into the idea of their religion. Wasn't Morning Star an angel favoured by God? In the eyes of the people, he was a demon now. Angel or demon, it was just a matter of semantics and perspectives.

'Why don't you show them?' Lady Nightshade urged Marguerite Daisy, the shit-stirrer that she was, keen to have both Ernest and the White Lotus ghost dead before she died of boredom herself. 'Make them suffer, I want to see some blood . . . their blood,' she said, her eyes gleaming wickedly.

Taking the Soul-keeper necklace by her hand, Marguerite Daisy flew to the night-blue sky where the stars were sown, hovering in mid-air while feeling the heaven above her and the cosmos within her. Invoking the soul of the old sea god Gatsasi the Great with a prayer using her pearl rosary, she turned scaly all over like a fish while tapping into his powers of aqua-kinesis— capable of exerting his dominion and control over water in all its myriad forms.

> All the seas are angry tonight,
> The tide is full, the moon glows fair.
> Perish this night with no help in sight,
> Drown in fear, make hell your lair.

Drops of rain fell as ice daggers onto the ground while the underground streams burst up like geysers, sending the White Lotus ghost and Ernest helter-skelter like headless chickens trying to protect themselves in a frenzied maelstrom of panic and confusion. Danger was everywhere and anywhere as white-water rapids swept them like tsunamis, gushing from every nook and cranny where they least expected them.

With what he thinks was Bomoh Mona Mawar's word of advice ringing in his ears, the White Lotus ghost saw Ernest believing into existence a bolt of lightning from his magic wand, and it hit Marguerite Daisy squarely on her chest—shocking her senseless as she fell onto the ground with a loud thud.

Watching in horror and screaming in denial, Lady Nightshade took out her tarot card like a whisper of a shadow's song and brought glory to the morning star beyond the cosmos at the far reaches of hell. She knew a psychic medium like herself could be a conduit to instigate the presence of a living evil, and she was hell-bent on doing so—she brought The Devil to all lives on earth!

'Behold, the Devil,' she screamed and raised the tarot card, hoping to turn the tide in her favour. The earth roared in pain as a storm of lightning rocked the mountains while reality cracked in protest at the presence of an unholy menace from beyond that turned everything dark like a spectre's soul, hiding much of heaven and earth from view. 'Hell is here and now; abandon all hope and pray for a quick death,' she yelled maniacally.

> My wings, they whisper, my horns they kill,
> War, pestilence, famine, and death I bring to you.
> Dark in the light of infinity, waiting for a kill,
> Fire, hell, pain, and suffering I wish unto you.

'Father, I bring you a sacrifice,' Marguerite Daisy hollered to The Devil as she raised Ernest by his neck in her Gatsasi avatar form. To the White Lotus ghost's utter dismay, he seemed rigid like rigor mortis had taken over—his blood frozen by Marguerite Daisy what it being a form of water and all, an element that was under her control. 'Your reign on earth begins,' said the daughter of The Devil as she laughed triumphantly, vain and proud like hell for all and sundry to witness.

'Very good, my daughter,' The Devil praised his halfling child as all hell broke loose. His mere presence in this plane of reality precipitated apocalypse in all its chaos, ushering in his legacy of blood and tears in all their unholy damnation and dominion.

War—the dead interred in tombs rose and marched asleep, as nightmares became reality when the Doomsday Clock began its final countdown with nuclear missiles preparing to launch themselves from around the world.

Pestilence—demonic pests of every kind crawled out of hell from the earth's bowels and took to the skies and seas in massive numbers without warning, sweeping across continents as they threatened fatal outbreaks of pandemics by contagion.

Famine—the dust storms kissed the furrowed, cracked earth as harvests died and lands were laid bare while raging fires raced across forests and farmlands. Worse still, the Styx from hell overflowed its banks and spilled its poisons into the earth's waterways.

Death—souls were ripped from bodies in an unholy rapture, causing airplanes to crash and cars to collide with each other while trains got derailed from their tracks and ships sank into their watery graves.

All was lost, plundered, defiled, and destroyed as the world plunged into pandemonium and immeasurable depths of sorrow. Looking at the devastation and desolation around, the White Lotus ghost's heart broke, as much as the sight of Ernest lay dying like that for trying to save her lost soul!

Her bravado was gone with the crushing of hope along with her faith until a silent scream went off in the empty dark of her heart, and sadness for her friend overwhelmed her . . . she would die for him as he lay dying for her.

No, no, no . . . they were losing the world and she was losing her only friend, she panicked inside out. Everything as they knew it came crashing down and dying into oblivion. No farewell to the wind, no goodbye to the sky. Laughter and breeze, kindness and seas, innocence and streams; all that was good, all that was him would be gone if she didn't do anything and The Devil got a final foothold in this plane of reality.

In a fit of desperation and anguish, she cried to the heavens above and hurled her BaShe fang sabre at Lady Nightshade— hitting her directly—right in her evil heart. With a sputter of blood from her lips, she unceremoniously fell onto the ground as poison took hold of her rotting corpse while her tarot card perished from her grasp for all time—sending The Devil back to whence he came from and ending the apocalypse in a blink of an eye.

'No, no, no . . .' the White Lotus ghost heard Marguerite Daisy protesting aloud and saw the latter losing her concentration . . . and her hold on Ernest. What the man saw upon waking up must have defrosted his frozen blood, and a burst of pure energy fuelled by his need for survival erupted from his magic wand and knocked out his hateful tormentor cold onto the floor.

Instinct drove him to take possession of the Soul-keeper pearl necklace lest Marguerite Daisy woke up and wreaked havoc with it—one Gatsasi avatar form from a single pearl had already done so much harm and he shuddered to think what the other souls of the old gods from the precious double-stranded necklace that she could tap into could do.

Damn it, The Devil's daughter was a veritable pantheon of the old gods unto herself . . . if she could crack all their prayer spells, that was. Very highly unlikely without her grandmother, Countess Wisteria Yates; her mother, Lady Madam Petunia Yates; or Lady Nightshade's help, she would assume.

'Are you alright, Pai Lian? You got me scared there for a moment,' Ernest said as he helped the White Lotus ghost get up on her feet, concerned that she was sustaining a lot of injuries. Seeing her smile despite her weakened state brought relief to him, now that their ordeal was almost over.

The White Lotus ghost could feel his heart brimming with joy at their victory—fighting the first wave of the apocalypse against all odds. It was a friendship from the opposite sides of fate, him a mortal being while she a ghost. By chance they met, by choice they became friends.

She shed a tear for a friendship separated by different realms; the stars in heaven were destined to be separated by vast distances and their friendship soon to be doomed by vast differences . . . across life and death.

She knew she should learn to live in an empty void and acquiesce herself to the embrace of emptiness and loneliness, though her tears already knew she was to forfeit her friendship with him for an eternal nightmare of torment and suffering for the sins she had accrued. Sadly, their partnership was a long goodbye and she had to endure the passing of his presence and the absence of her going, across the far reaches of time, never to be friends again.

Her face tried putting on a brave front, a mask of lie to hide the loss in her heart and the tears in her eyes—thinking of the debts she had to pay for her guiles and wiles with her bleeding soul while she waited for the inevitable . . . the arrival of the deities of impermanence, the Heibai Wuchang guardians from the netherworld.

> A single tear, a hundred cries, a thousand fears,
> Hell is sweltering with the heat of your sins.
> Sink deeper right into hell, annihilation is near,
> Forget salvation, there's no redemption no win.

A fire storm from the deepest pits of hell erupted as both Heibai Wuchang guardians rose again and roared with fury—releasing their long, long tongues of red simultaneously as their black and white shadows traversed the land and warped the reality around them, expending justice.

Lady Nightshade went quietly into the night as her lifeless body pungent with sins was dragged into the intoxicating darkness of hell most unceremoniously. Her soul never to come back to the realm of the living; her evil never to return and haunt the heavenly paradise that she so secretly desired to call home.

Bomoh Mona Mawar became a spirit of the rose garden here on earth, capable of taking on humanly forms whenever she pricked her soul with a thorn from her rose bushes. Her beauty was no longer dependent on *jarum susuk* golden needles; her kindness to handsome young men lost in her rose garden at midnight grew with her legend.

Marguerite Daisy, while not dead, got justice served to her as well—she was imprisoned in a limbo outside of space and time for her misdeeds; bound in chains unbreakable, her soul torn and her sanity broken. As darkness called to her and light faded away from her cell, she screamed and screamed in madness before silence reigned in her tongue and violence burst from her heart waiting for the day her father, The Devil, came and rescued her.

As for the White Lotus ghost, she hugged a crying Ernest goodbye as she traversed the Naihe Bridge, safe from hellish tribulations to her next rebirth—her dearest friend had secured her deliverance with the exchange of the precious artefacts in his name; the magic wand from The Magician, and the accursed South Sea pearl necklace from Marguerite Daisy, which were all his by right of conquest.

The White Lotus ghost had never known true friendship until this man whom she had saved from suicide fell to his knees and wept at the feet of the deities of impermanence for her safe salvation. He reasoned on bloodied knees that they had done enough to avert Armageddon to merit an exchange.

Providence had been kind to him, but he gave everything he had for her. Unfortunately, fate was unkind to him—he had to live with this memory of them while she would have the blessing of Granny Meng Po's Broth of Oblivion to start anew.

> My friend, with the rise of the setting sun,
> I'm breaking apart as we kiss goodbye.
> The memories, the foolish times, the fun,
> Leave them behind with tears in our eyes.

27

15 January 1980

After Ernest had finished signing the last book for the day at a book reading event in the Taiping Botanical Garden, he looked up at the beaming faces of his adoring fans, their numbers growing day by day with every favourable review from the critics. His book had not only baffled them and the press, it had also made it to the shortlist of various prestigious awards already. Once ridiculed as an utter failure, Ernest was now a successful bestselling author, and the book had even outsold *A Bridge to Murderville*.

After the event, Ernest walked to the bridge. It was already late evening. Under the bright full moon sky, thoughts flooded him as he gazed at the floating lotuses, bringing with them a rush of tears for a friendship lost to fate. He stood there reminiscing the turn of events that had changed the tide of his fate.

The ladies under the bridge were all gone, having crossed the Naihe Bridge to new lives beyond his reach. Now, it had fallen unto him, the burden and the release of their memories flowing within the pond's waters, wondering when it would be his turn to cross the rainbow bridge to the thereafter.

Forever and ever, as the pond of lotuses glowed under the gaze of the heavenly stars, his heart would always be touched by recollections of the lives and deaths of the Chang sisters.

As the white lotuses rose from the mud below to bloom above in the open, his heart would forever be thankful for his ghostwriter who had made him a huge success.

It wasn't just him, Inspector Abdul Rahman was thankful too, having gotten his promotion and pay raise for solving the biggest case of his lifetime. Rumours had it that he built a house with his windfall in a mysterious garden full of beautiful roses.

'I want to thank you, my friend, for the story of a lifetime,' Ernest said to the lotuses beneath the bridge, his heart brimming with gratitude. He had grown as a writer, thanks to Chang Pai Lian, and would be starting work on a new book—*Horror, He Wrote 2: The Witch at the Bell Tower*—a sequel to ride on the resounding success of his first bestseller. 'Come hell or high water, I'll finish the book on my own and make you proud.'

The lotuses and their broken reflections,
and their shadows below the moon;
Live forever as a symbol of his passion,
until the time for them to meet soon.